Thea Welsh is the author of the prize winning novel *The Story of the Year of 1912 in the Village of Elza Darzins*, and *Welcome Back*. She lives in Sydney with her partner and, from time to time, three cats.

THE CAT WHO LOOKED AT THE SKY

A MEMOIR

Thea Welsh

flamingo
An imprint of HarperCollins*Publishers*

Flamingo
An imprint of HarperCollinsPublishers

First published in Australia in 2003
Reprinted in 2003
by HarperCollins*Publishers* Pty Limited
ABN 36 009 913 517
A member of the HarperCollins*Publishers* (Australia) Pty Limited Group
www.harpercollins.com.au

Copyright © Edgecliff Media Pty Ltd 2003

The right of Thea Welsh to be identified as the moral rights author of
this work has been asserted by her in accordance with the
Copyright Amendment (Moral Rights) Act 2000 (Cth).

This book is copyright.
Apart from any fair dealing for the purposes of private study, research,
criticism or review, as permitted under the Copyright Act, no part may
be reproduced by any process without written permission.
Inquiries should be addressed to the publishers.

HarperCollins*Publishers*
25 Ryde Road, Pymble, Sydney NSW 2073, Australia
31 View Road, Glenfield, Auckland 10, New Zealand
77–85 Fulham Palace Road, London W6 8JB, United Kingdom
2 Bloor Street East, 20th floor, Toronto, Ontario M4W 1A8, Canada
10 East 53rd Street, New York NY 10022, USA

National Library of Australia Cataloguing-in-publication data:

Welsh, Thea.
  The cat who looked at the sky.
  ISBN 0 7322 7617 9.
  1. Cats 2. Cat owners 3. Human–animal relationships I. Title.
636.80887

Cover photograph of Grace by Michael Thornhill
Cover design by Gayna Murphy, HarperCollins Design Studio
Internal design by Louise McGeachie
Typeset in Giovanni Book 10/15pt by HarperCollins Design Studio
Printed and bound in Australia by Griffin Press on 70gsm Bulky Book Ivory

6 5 4 3 2   03 04 05 06

For Robin

CONTENTS

SUMMER
Serial Cats 2
Fruit Bats on Speed 12
Securing the Targets 19
Aerial Wars 26
The Academy 35

AUTUMN
AKAs 46
The Cat's Whiskers 55
She-Who-Was-Kate 64
Violins and Snow in the Streets 72

WINTER
Biker Toms 82
The Marching Season 89
Men Who Fall In Love With Cats 98
The Arrival of Gravy 110

SPRING
Wash 'n' Wrestle 124
Real Estate 136
Theme Parks for Cats 143
Cocktail Hour 155

SUMMER/AUTUMN
Thug Princess 168
Kinky and Diverse 181
New Stern Regime 202
Temple Cat 222

ONE YEAR LATER
The Cat Who Looked at the Sky 234
Epilogue 260

SUMMER

SERIAL CATS

I often think that along with all that data cats are said to have pre-wired into their brains about how to raise kittens, do their laundry and be a predator, they also have a principle made famous by Jane Austen when she adapted it to the human context: it's a truth universally acknowledged that a household not in possession of a dog must be in want of a cat.

Until we got the kittens, I'd never made an arrangement to acquire a cat. They used to arrive in my life simply by appearing at my door. After several years of this I had come to believe there was a whole strata of cats in the inner suburbs of Sydney who understood my circumstances perfectly. They knew I loved cats but thought it irresponsible to get one when I wasn't sure I could offer it a permanent home. At the same time they were aware I didn't see anything wrong in helping out if a cat decided — for whatever reasons of its own — that it

Summer

needed somewhere different to live or maybe just to spend its afternoons.

I was never particular about the terms of these arrangements. I got along happily with visitors who always called by at meal times and with others who only dropped in on weekends. For periods of up to a year, I provided an alternative household for a series of cats who would have considered it positively eccentric to reside full time at the one address. Although I was always sad when the current cat decided to move on, I accepted it as part of the deal and remember being more impressed than upset when one of my semi-resident friends advised of his impending departure by public notice.

I was in my local supermarket at the time. I'd been absent-mindedly perusing the community noticeboard and was pushing my trolley down the aisle when I suddenly did a classic slapstick-comedy double-take. On the board there'd been a handwritten notice declaring, "FOUND: Large male ginger cat, with white paws, very affectionate." It was the underlining that did it. Large male ginger cats with white paws aren't that uncommon and it hadn't occurred to me until that point that Geoffrey George Gregory could be considered lost. After all, he'd been devotedly occupying three-quarters of my bed every night as usual. But it was clear now that he'd been taking serious steps about moving into somebody else's house during the day.

My years of living with serial cats came to a halt with Pusscat. Well, to be accurate, they came to a halt for me. Pusscat herself never really gave up her aspirations to acquire a new household or, preferably, several new households simultaneously, until she became too frail to take all the journeys around the neighbourhood that locating these additional homes required.

By this time Michael and I are living together. We have moved into a house in Paddington which, in socio-economic terms, is a cut above the suburbs where I'd been living previously. Without thinking much about it, I assume therefore that the cats of Paddington are also a cut above cats of my previous acquaintance. They look the part. I'm used to cats who scrounge out of garbage bins, run down back alleys and peer at you apprehensively as you pass. These cats recline on iron lace balconies, promenade through Tuscan-style courtyards and accept pats from French and Japanese tourists on the weekends.

So when Pusscat appears at our door, wailing for admittance, it doesn't occur to me that she's a serial cat and first cousin (probably several times over) to half a dozen other cats with whom I've had relationships in tougher locales. Instead I decide she's seriously neglected at home and let her take up residence. The fact that she, after successfully managing the move into our house, keeps on trying to move into other houses doesn't make me view her any more realistically. I just ascribe her chronic unfaithfulness to an unhappy childhood.

When Pusscat dies, I'm so used to a succession of serial cats arriving and adopting me that I simply wait for her successor to appear. I expect this process will take longer than in less affluent areas because there don't seem to be any homeless cats around, but I'm sure it will happen. I suspect there's some sort of feline network that passes the news of vacant homes along so that one day I'll come out my back door and find a cat I've never seen before sitting quietly on the fence. The next stage of the process, the transition from stranger to resident cat, may take hours or days or weeks but that doesn't concern me. I'm just impatient for my new cat to arrive.

In the meantime I imagine wistfully what the new cat will be like. It will have soft, silver-grey fur and a beautiful face with markings a little reminiscent of a tiger's. It will be sociable and affectionate. It will purr on my lap while I watch TV and sleep on my bed in winter and it will be particularly fond of dinner parties during which it will station itself next to a susceptible guest who'll feed it tidbits. In other words, as I realise one day, I expect my new cat to be exactly like Pusscat.

That's when I know that I have to start thinking about different sorts of cats. Black cats, brown cats, big cats, small cats … I'm thinking about small cats when it occurs to me that I'd like to get a cat with a kitten. I think it would be interesting watching a kitten grow, and after years of living with cats still suffering the ill-effects of tough childhoods, I feel it would be satisfying to raise a properly cared for cat. By the time this idea gets announced to Michael, it's been expanded to a cat and two kittens. I always felt sorry for Pusscat being on her own and think it would be nice to have two cats for company. In my mind's eye I see two fluffy black and white kittens washing each other's ears with little pink tongues.

But Michael is not keen. Long before we met he had a cat called Mothercat who, unsurprisingly in view of her name, had kittens. These offspring turned out to be trouble. One got attacked by a dog and had to have its leg put in splints and be found a new home in a distant suburb. Another was always getting itself stuck in places and the others were just generally demanding in ways he couldn't exactly recall. Although I was disappointed by his opposition, I was secretly very pleased by this story. During all the time that Pusscat had lived with us, Michael had held the late Mothercat up to me as such an example of a loyal, loving and intelligent cat that I was delighted now to learn this paragon had managed to produce kittens so delinquent that he wouldn't hear of having another pair twenty years later.

"They're just too much to look after," he says.

"But we wouldn't have to look after them," I reply, still happily contemplating my two imaginary black and white kittens. "That's why we would have a mother cat."

He doesn't point out how much sheer ignorance of kitten-raising this remark conveys. All the cats of my adult years have been adult cats. I had grown up on a farm where there'd been litters of kittens but they were cared for by their mothers and, in my recollections, the main dramas seemed to have been about giving birth. For weeks in advance of the deliveries, my mother would be shooing pregnant cats out of linen cupboards and trying to re-route them to the lying-in beds we'd prepared. The last batch of farm kittens we'd had before I left home were semi-ferals. They lived in the garden shed and though my parents gave them food, most afternoons the little mother cat went off hunting. Around sunset she and her offspring would share an alfresco dinner of rabbit under the bushes in the rose garden. In retrospect it's obvious this

Summer

experience equipped me about as much for raising kittens as driving past a pre-school would fit you out for parenthood.

After this I forget about getting kittens and go back to waiting wistfully for my new cat to arrive (by this stage I'm up to exchanging significant glances with every cat within a three mile radius in the hope that either it will come home with me or it will let its mates know there's a vacancy in the neighbourhood.) But, as I soon discover, Michael remembers our conversation. At the start of summer I go to the country to visit my family. When I return he comes to the airport to collect me and on our way home astonishes me by casually announcing he's had a talk the previous evening with our friends, Ron and Robin, about the four of us jointly adopting a pair of kittens.

Ron is an American while Robin is Australian. Ron works as a graphic designer in films and for over twenty years they have lived in California. But they have come to Australia frequently and had finally decided, about twelve months previously, to base themselves in Sydney.

When I ask later whose idea it had been that we should adopt the kittens together, it turned out that neither Michael nor Ron nor Robin could remember. Indeed, as none of them seem to have retained any recollection of the entire conversation, I develop the following scenario: Ron and Robin have come to dinner with Michael. At some point in the evening, they start talking cats. This is a sad topic. It's the first time they've been to our house since Pusscat died. They were used to her sitting on the windowsill by the dining table, accepting homage (she looked very pretty by candlelight) and cadging treats. Also, I suspect they are still mourning their own favourite cat, Norton, who died in California the year before at the age of twenty. I never met Norton but Michael would come back from Los Angeles with stories of his intelligence and prowess. Ron and Robin had a number of cats over the years but Norton was the special one. He was clever, affectionate and beautiful, possessed of special skills and personality, the legendary cat.

Ron and Robin haven't got a cat since arriving in Sydney because, as Robin explains, the best cats they've had are those, like Norton, whom they have raised from kittens. They have to go back to the States frequently, though, for Ron's work and don't feel they can go away for unpredictable periods of time and leave small kittens with strange households or parked in catteries. Maybe it's at this point that Michael remarks that Thea was talking about wanting to get a pair of kittens and Robin reiterates that it's the only way to be sure of getting a cat that hasn't been damaged in some way. This leads to a number of cautionary tales about adult cats they have adopted who turned out to have textbook-case personality disorders or developed diseases so expensive that Robin found it advisable to start playing tennis on a weekly basis with their vet. Then maybe Robin makes the critical suggestion. Or perhaps the idea occurs to both her and Michael simultaneously.

Either way, by the end of dinner the details are worked out. If I agree to the scheme, Robin and Ron will get two kittens who will live between the two houses, with two sets of owners. As they're usually in Los Angeles every couple of

Summer

months for anything from two to eight weeks, we can expect to have the cats for roughly half the year. Michael is happy to waive his objections to kittens since Ron and Robin have had so much experience raising them.

When Michael tells me about the plan, I am very surprised. I have never heard of anyone agreeing to co-own cats before, though I've known quite a number of cats who ran parallel households. The random bits of feline lore that I've acquired suggest that cats are highly territorial and don't like change but I figure if the kittens are used to transiting from one house to the other from the start, then they'll regard it as normal. Also, experience has made me sceptical of a number of things I've been told or have read about cats.

For example, I'd often heard that cats are loners. But after living with a succession of them on and off for fifteen years, I have come to the conclusion that either I've met an unrepresentative sample or I attracted the especially sociable ones because all of the cats with whom I had a close acquaintance were gregarious to the point of "I know it's only mid-morning, but why don't we open a nice bottle of white and ring around and see who's free for lunch?" I usually got deserted when I had to take a job to finance my writing career. Once the current cat discovered that I was no longer at home all the time, there was none of that sentimental nonsense about waiting loyally for me to come back from my paid employment in the evenings. I guess in cats' perceptions, cities are full of people who abandon them for hours each day. Instead the current cat would promptly start looking around for another household which could provide it with more constant company.

Once I recover from my surprise at Michael's news, I say it's a wonderful idea. My memory bank immediately revives my two imaginary kittens, all sweetly fluffy with their black and white patches, sitting contentedly side by side and occasionally washing each other's ears. I'm so used to serial cats coming and going that sharing ownership doesn't worry me. Indeed, I almost regard it as the norm. It wasn't so long ago that I happened to remark during drinks with some neighbours, "Pusscat usually sleeps on our bed once the cold weather starts, but she doesn't seem interested this year." There was a pause. Afterwards I felt foolish for not having realised earlier where Pusscat had been spending her nights.

Over another dinner, the kitten deal is finalised. None of us is interested in acquiring cats of exotic breeds or with distinguished pedigrees when there are always abandoned kittens needing homes, so it's agreed that Robin will go to the local vet's surgery where there are usually cats for adoption and select two kittens. Ideally she and Ron want the new cats to be like Norton — both affectionate and intelligent — but they're prepared to welcome whatever is available at the vet's. Their only stipulation is that we must get kittens who are used to being handled. Michael and I say this sounds perfect.

Michael, Ron and I are also very happy to leave the actual business of selection to Robin. Ron excuses himself from the mission on the grounds that he'd want to bring home every available cat. Michael trusts Robin's judgment and I don't think I'm equipped to choose a cat. I keep remembering a conversation from years before when I'd asked Robin how she and Ron had acquired Norton.

"We went to the vet's where they had some kittens that needed homes."

"Yes, but why did you choose him?"

"There was one black kitten which was running and jumping and looking alert and so we took him home with us. That was Norton."

I was very impressed by this but also taken aback. I had been prepared to help fate along when I guessed there was a cat in the offing by leaving windows open and putting bowls of food in strategic locations. But actually going and selecting a cat was so different from my experience that it felt like an arranged marriage.

FRUIT BATS ON SPEED

Ron and Robin ring one evening in early December to announce the two kittens have finally been chosen and are now in residence at their place. "One's brown, one's black," says Robin. "The black one is fluffy," she goes on, "we think the other's part Burmese."

"Oh," I say, surprised. And a little disappointed. I had expected siblings. Without thinking about it, I'd somehow assumed kittens got conveniently abandoned in family groups. If we didn't get my ideal black and white kittens, I had expected two decorative little cats who resembled one another.

In the background I can hear Ron saying excitedly, "They're running. They're jumping. They're eating. They're purring. They're playing. They're climbing. They're tearing about."

I can see now I would have been wise to take some notice of his verb-laden description because, as I was soon

Summer

to discover, real six-week-old kittens are an action movie while my imaginary black and white ones were a period romance. But at the time I decide that I don't want to hear anything further about the new arrivals. My overactive imagination has already gotten me into trouble by inventing my ideal kittens. I want to meet the real ones without developing more preconceptions.

Two weeks later, the kittens arrive at our place for their first visit, as Ron and Robin have to go to Melbourne for a few days. It's a hot afternoon and Michael and I decide that we'll have drinks to welcome them on the shady upstairs balcony that overlooks the street. This balcony is off the sitting room. We know that the kittens should be introduced to their new environment gradually so we have decided that the sitting room will function initially as their nursery. After they've become accustomed to it, they can start exploring the rest of the house.

The newcomers are carried in with what seems to me an impressive amount of paraphernalia — pet carrier; litter trays; food dishes; tins, bags and boxes of food and back-up supplies of kitty litter. The kittens emerge from their carrier to be introduced and for maybe the first few seconds they are tentative. But after that they begin to move and my general memory of that first short visit is of two tiny individuals, the size of the palm of my hand, who are in non-stop motion. They leap, they jump, they climb, they whirl, they spin on their back legs and on occasion, presumably because they've exhausted the resources of teams of internal choreographers, they merely run.

"It's also a very quick trip," Robin comments as Michael and I are gazing at the two small bodies careering rapidly past us, "from their mouths to their bottoms." But this considerably understates the matter because it emerges that the kittens can eat, shit and fly almost simultaneously. With a bound from a chair, they'll land by a food dish, swallow a rapid mouthful, then leap onto the litter tray, pause, and be scrambling up onto a table a whole quarter of a second later.

As I watch them I become aware of how wrong my preconceptions have been. My imaginary black and white kittens were cute and charming. Nothing like these real-life specimens who are always charging, fleeing, attacking, retreating and tumbling in a fight across the floor. Being decorative doesn't come into it. They are like fruit bats on speed.

Robin starts explaining how she came to select the kittens. There were no homeless cats at the local vet's and she had been referred to a another surgery where there were half a dozen kittens for adoption in a wire pen. The kittens consisted of one small black fluffy one, all of whose siblings had already been adopted, and another family of five who appeared to be some sort of Burmese-tabby mix. The fluffy black one had golden eyes and was very pretty. By contrast the Burmese-tabby litter were an unattractive bunch. Robin reports that they were pawing and biting and thrusting each other away from the food dishes.

If I hadn't been aware how prone the fluffy black kitten was at this stage of her life to leap upon an object simply because an object to leap upon had presented itself, I would have thought she recognised immediately that Robin was her ticket out of living with this mean and

Summer

nasty family because, as Robin knelt down for a closer look, what the fluffy black kitten did was to suddenly leap straight up onto her shoulder. Robin cupped her hand around the small black body and made her first choice.

"Right," she said. "You're in."

She held the black kitten and sat down to review her pen mates. On closer study, the Burmese-tabby siblings didn't look any more appealing. But there were no other options, so she decided to conduct a serious audition. She tells us that for half an hour she sat and watched the Burmese-tabby kittens play and she eventually noticed that one of the kittens seemed nicer than the others. It was not as aggressive as its siblings, it looked bright and alert, and it seemed very interested in and curious about its surroundings. So she decided to adopt it and that is how the brown part-Burmese kitten arrives in our lives.

At this point Ron takes over the narrative. "The first morning after we got them," he says, leaning down to stroke the brown kitten as she flies past him, "I carried her outside to take a photograph and she looked straight up at the sky. There wasn't a bird flying over or anything for her to watch. She just saw it was there. She's the first cat I've ever seen look at the sky."

It's obvious that at that moment he decided the brown kitten was special and fell in love with her. I can see that for Ron and Robin, relations with the kittens are going swimmingly. Robin was enchanted by the black kitten when it leapt on her shoulder, Ron was captivated by the brown one when she looked up at the sky. At the same time both Ron and Robin adore the kitten with whom they haven't yet fallen in love. There's no need for jealousy or competition. Every member of the foursome, cat and human, is happy.

However, I'm not doing so well. I'd been expecting to fall in love with both kittens the minute I met them, yet I don't seem to be forming a bond with either of them. Even then it's apparent that they have very different personalities. Black Kitten is affectionate. She likes cuddles and has short sleeps in the curve of an arm or across Robin's shoulder. Brown Kitten is more reserved. She accepts pats but mostly she's watchful, gazing at us unfamiliar human beings with big bright eyes set in a tiny triangle of a face dominated by triangular ears so disproportionately large — especially on top of that tiny face — as to be listening stations for Mars.

Of course, I say the kittens are gorgeous but to be honest I'm disappointed. If you had asked me at that first meeting what I really thought of them, I would have said that they were two of the least cat-like creatures I'd ever seen. In my view Brown Kitten resembles a rat with big ears who has been to a bad furrier. Her tan and black coat is patterned so erratically, it looks like a rug that has run in the wash. Also, she's got a pale pinkish-brown stripe up the middle of her nose which instead of being a neat straight line, peters off to one side at the top as though whoever was responsible had a few drinks while doing the finishing touches to her face.

I can see why the others think the black kitten is pretty — she has a pure black coat and golden eyes with black liquid centres like million-dollar jewellery. But I find the contrast between the light-coloured eyes and her coat extreme. Also, I keep feeling there's something strange

Summer

about her. In fact if it had been discovered shortly afterwards that she was actually a member of some obscure species of black-haired monkey who in their early lives are commonly mistaken for cats, I wouldn't have been at all surprised.

But I know that part of the reason I'm so unresponsive to the kittens is because I'm comparing them unfavourably to another cat. One afternoon, a couple of weeks previously, while Michael was working at his desk, a big white cat ran into his office, leapt onto his lap and started to purr. By the time I meet the white cat, Michael has found out who he is. Two pleasant young brothers are renting the house next door. The white cat belongs to their parents who have recently sold the family home and moved into an apartment, so the family cat has come to live with our neighbours.

Or, to be more accurate, with us. Once Mr White Cat discovers there is constant company at our house, while his official carers are often out, he decides to relocate. He makes it clear he thinks we are wonderful. We even have a cupboard full of cat food for him because Pusscat died suddenly and I have never had the heart to dispose of it, just as I've never been able to go the vet's and reclaim the pet carrier in which she had made her final trip.

Michael and I are just as impressed with him as he is with us. His manner is very self-assured. He's completely different from Pusscat who wailed outside our door until we gave in and adopted her. Instead, he gives the impression of being a well-heeled cat with a full and busy life — meetings with his broker, lunches at the club with rels down from the country, fundraisers for his old school

— which makes it all the more delightful that he can squeeze in the time to come and visit us. Eventually we learn his official name but by then we have already christened him, Il Gato Blanco, after a Chilean wine everyone is drinking that summer. We soon shorten this to GB. He's an initials sort of cat. We are sure he drives a BMW.

It never occurs to me in advance that GB might find our part ownership of the kittens a problem. He's such a calm, sociable urbane cat that I imagine him being a sort of kindly uncle to the new arrivals. Giving them an occasional wash and stopping them from doing themselves damage. But the instant the kittens emerge from their carrier, GB leaves the house. I run after him and call him back. In the end I carry him upstairs and Ron sits down on the floor with him, holding him gently and trying to soothe him and talk him into staying. But GB is having none of it. As soon as Ron releases him, he hurries out of the house. I have a feeling that in his eyes, I've committed some social lapse so awful he can't bear to have it mentioned.

Now, as I gaze at Brown Kitten who resembles a rat and Black Kitten whom I think could be a monkey, I find I am beginning to feel distinctly in sympathy with GB. I'm not sure I want this unexpected duo around either. As an arranged marriage, this is a misfire. Belatedly I realise that what we needed was two mature, sensible cats capable of looking after themselves and of managing Michael and me. Instead we've got a pair of high-powered infant delinquents with hyperactivity syndromes and attention-deficit disorders. I'm relieved the relationship is only going to be part time.

SECURING THE TARGETS

Our first night of kitten care is hot and steamy. Michael and I are so anxious about the new arrivals, we decide we will keep them in the sitting room. It's large enough for them to play in and there are several chairs, a sofa and a coffee table which they can leap onto, or climb up onto, or use as helipads. When we are with them we can also open the French doors onto the balcony. For the first few hours of our watch things go well but, inevitably, just when we're about to go to bed, there's a crisis.

I'm in the shower at the time and through the running water, I hear Michael calling to me urgently: "One of them's missing!"

I bustle out of the bathroom, a towel wrapped quickly around me, leaving wet footprints on the hall carpet. "Which one?"

"The brown one, of course," says Michael wearily. "She's the intellectual," he adds, as if this is a perfectly ordinary thing to say about a six-week-old kitten.

He's looking hot and agitated. He thinks the missing kitten might have slipped out onto the balcony when he went out quickly for some air, but he can't find her there or anywhere in the room. He's frightened that she has taken a leap over the balcony wall and is now dead down in the street. He's been down to search but —

"Where's the other one?" I interrupt, looking around. I suspect that Ron and Robin's stance on the loss of kittens will be the same as Lady Bracknell's on losing parents. Losing one is unfortunate. Losing two looks like carelessness.

"She was here a minute ago."

At this point Black Kitten obligingly appears from underneath a chair. I've seen enough movies about the secret service and presidential assassination plots to know what to do next. Secure the target. I quickly scoop her up.

"Put her in the pet carrier," I say, passing the kitten to Michael and beginning my own search of the sitting room. I'm the designated finder of the household. I often lose things when I start thinking about writing and become absent-minded, but my recovery rate is well above Michael's. The black kitten meanwhile is getting agitated, wriggling her little body in panic, trying to escape from Michael's grip as he fiddles with the plastic clasps on the front of the pet carrier. He's as upset as she is. It's obvious to him just how much Ron adores the brown kitten and here we are, only hours into our first stint as kitten carers, and she's gone AWOL. Perhaps terminally.

"I can't get it open," he says in exasperation.

Michael's much more mechanically minded than I am

Summer

and it's not often I get the opportunity to upstage him in this regard. In the midst of the crisis I admit I take a fair amount of pleasure in saying quellingly, "I don't think you need to be a rocket scientist to open a cat carrier."

Despite Brown Kitten's tiny size, there are not that many places in either the lounge room or on the balcony where she could conceal herself. There are two bookcases double-packed with books, three chairs, the sofa, the coffee table and a desk. On the balcony there is only a table and a few chairs. I systematically examine every piece of furniture, behind and underneath, but I can't find Brown Kitten anywhere. Then I pull on some clothes and go down to inspect the street.

Once I'm there another problem becomes apparent. The street trees cast dark shadows over the footpath, street and gutter. Inevitably our torch batteries are flat and it's soon obvious that the only way I could locate Brown Kitten's small body in the darkness would be by stepping on it. Nonetheless I wander around despondently for a few minutes hoping I might hear a little cry. I have just decided that we'll have to wait until morning to mount a search party when Michael suddenly calls over the balcony, "She's back!"

I hurry into the house and up the stairs. "Where did you find her?"

"I turned around," he says, "and there she was. She was just standing there." He points to a spot by the French doors.

"Where is she now?"

There's no Brown Kitten in view. I'm worried she might have de-materialised just as quickly as she reappeared. He

The Cat Who Looked at the Sky

indicates the pet carrier where two tiny faces are now gazing at us. I have a feeling he's thinking that it would be simpler for us and safer for them if the kittens spend all their time within its confines.

This is the first time we see Brown Kitten manifest that famous feline skill called "appearing out of nowhere". Afterwards we decide that she hid herself that night by going to sleep on the arm of a chair on the balcony. The chair had been pushed a short way under the table creating a tiny space, just big enough for a very small kitten, between the chair arm and the table. We had checked the seat of the chair. We had checked under the table. We had checked under the chair. It just hadn't occurred to us to check the ends of the arms of the chair that were under the table.

In later searches we model ourselves on those forensic scientists on TV who can identify the killer after discovering a fragment of a sub-Saharan grass seed at the murder site. But we never quite lose our nervousness about the brown kitten's ability to disappear. During the kittens' next few visits, whenever either of us returns to the house and gets met in the front hall only by the black kitten, we first say "Hello, darling," followed promptly by an anxious "Where's your sister?" After a time I think the black kitten concludes we believe she is of Polish extraction and have named her "Warzyorcista".

The kittens' first tour of duty in their second home only lasts five hot days. I'm at work during the day so most of the caring is done by Michael, who goes upstairs from his office to the sitting room for regular familiarisation

Summer

sessions with the tiny newcomers. I even get exempted from caregiver duties in the evening because I'm soon allocated a more important task — keeping GB happy.

That very first evening, after our missing kitten crisis is resolved, Michael comes into our room, sits down heavily on the bed and says, "I want GB."

I sit down next to him nodding in sad agreement. We both imagine how things might have been: us reading quietly in bed, GB purring companionably or staging a leisurely wash in his chosen corner of the bed and looking calm and relaxed and elegant — especially when compared to these pint-sized feline flying foxes now occupying our sitting room. But after his exit GB has refused to reappear, even though I've gone to the dining room windows, which overlook the back garden, every quarter hour and called to him. We've begun to feel that he's abandoned us in outrage and is never coming back.

There's no sign of him next morning, but that evening just as it becomes dark, I see a white figure move in the shadows at the end of the garden, and I call to him. A minute later he's resettling himself on his favourite chair. No further attempts are made to introduce him to the newcomers. He's as affectionate towards Michael and me as ever, but as far as the kittens are concerned, the situation is like one of those period melodramas where the stern father refuses henceforth to ever hear mention of the name of the defaulting offspring.

Moreover GB, who has previously slept on our bed, dozed in the sitting room and joined company on the upstairs front balcony, now acts as though the entire upper floor of the house does not exist. Even when the kittens are gone, it's days before I can coax him up the stairs and even then he will never go towards the front part of the house where their odour must linger. I'm just at the stage where I think I can talk him into joining us in the bedroom again when he suddenly disappears out of our lives as quickly as he had entered them.

Michael says what happened is that one morning early in the New Year after I'd gone to work, he heard a woman calling for GB. He recognised the voice. Over Christmas our young neighbours had often been away and their parents had come around to feed GB and check on his welfare. This was the mother calling.

We had already noticed that GB had a thing about women. When the young men from next door called to him, he'd cock an ear but ignore them. But when their female visitors called his name, he would rise to his feet, and give us an apologetic look. Better see what the dear girl wants. And head off to his official home.

"I suddenly had a bad feeling," Michael tells me afterwards. "GB's ears were pricked up. I could see he didn't want to go. He was in his favourite chair, he was settling in for a big sleep. But he got up and went."

Although we don't realise it at the time, this was to be his final exit. Initially we are told that he's only going to be away for a few weeks, he is being taken to the family's holiday house up the coast. The parents have become anxious about him. They were worried, they tell us later, because he's been wandering a lot.

"Wandering" as applied to cats and husbands has long been one of my favourite euphemisms because it gives the impression of sweetly aimless roaming, whereas you

Summer

know in fact that the husbands and the cats have been hightailing it over the fence (quite literally in the case of the cats), deadset on adultery. But it's clearly not the time to start discussing the ironies of English language usage with GB's owners. Also, we are obviously not the right people to do so.

Instead we nod politely. It's all very civilised and friendly. They never imply there was anything the slightest bit untoward in our relationship with their cat, and we never point out that their cat has been sent away in disgrace because it was plainly intending to move house. Months later we hear that GB has returned to the city and is living with our neighbours' parents in their new house about a mile away. This is near a shopping centre where I often go, and for months afterwards, every time I am there I look around for GB. But I never see him. Eventually he passes into our household folklore along with Pusscat, and in time I realise this is appropriate because what he did was to help us cease mourning for her. Until he appeared, I couldn't really imagine life with another cat.

AERIAL WARS

"They've grown," announces Robin, delivering the kittens back to our care in the second half of January. "They are so much bigger!"

It's still early in the morning, I'm on my way to work, she and Ron are doing final things before leaving for Los Angeles, and they're running late. I'm gazing at the kittens thinking, grown? Bigger? Relative to what? Premature mice? To my eyes the duo still look minute. I estimate that they've expanded in size by maybe half an inch.

"I think you will also find them a bit calmer than before Christmas," she adds. I have my doubts about that too but reflect that now, at least, I know what to expect.

The kittens are old enough now to live throughout the house so they are let out of their pet carrier in the hall between the kitchen and Michael's office. Ron lays out food dishes, litter tray and water while Michael, Robin and I watch them through the glass hall door. Brown

Summer

Kitten is looking around her. The black kitten starts investigating the food dishes. Michael and I come out, one at a time, to kneel down by them, say hello and give them a pat. We then rejoin Ron and Robin in the office to receive our instructions. Most of the concern is about Brown Kitten. She is the adventurous one and it's clear that she's already eager to go exploring.

"If she makes it through to a year," Robin says to us while Ron goes back into the hall for a last goodbye with the kittens, "we think she'll survive."

We know this is meant to be reassuring. If the brown kitten dies in our care, Ron and Robin will regard it as fate and attach no blame. But it makes Michael and me look at her apprehensively. The front door onto the street is always closed but there is a lane behind the house which cars occasionally use and there are big trees, big dogs, big — well, big everything, actually, when you compare Brown Kitten's tiny body to anything else in our neighbourhood.

Meanwhile Robin's getting worried. "Come on, Ron," she says, opening the glass door. "We're very late. What are you doing?"

Ron is in the hall still, bent over the kittens. "Giving them the word," he says sadly as he straightens up.

My heart turns over. I promise Ron that I will write him a long letter and tell him all about the kittens. I also become determined that the kittens and Brown Kitten, in particular, are not going to die while they're with us. But as I'm thinking this, every possible danger in our inner-city environment — from garbage trucks to Great Danes — stages a rapid appearance in my imagination and

The Cat Who Looked at the Sky

executes a kitten. As we go out to the street to say goodbye to our friends, it strikes me that their Rozelle house is really a much safer environment for the joint kittens.

I say to Robin as she and Ron are getting into their car, "You don't get much traffic in your street. do you? There are not as many cars coming through as here."

"It only takes one, Thea," says Robin dryly as she buckles up her seat belt.

There's no comeback to this sensible observation. I know that Ron and Robin had a couple of cats run over during their time in Los Angeles.

The same thing must have been passing through Michael's mind because as we go back inside he says, "Fenwick, one of the cats they had in Los Angeles, got taken by a coyote."

We look at each other in relief. Whatever you can say about the streets of Paddington, there are no coyotes.

I have to leave immediately afterwards for work. I return home in the evening eager for news.

"How are they?"

Michael looks serious. "They're not happy. They chased each other up and down the stairs until they got exhausted and then they went out on the balcony, which they could remember from last time, and slept on one of the chairs. They're not happy," he says again. "I think it's been too long between visits."

I begin to feel worried but then remind myself that Michael's predictions often tend to be gloomy. I resolve to be positive. I tell myself it's inevitable that the kittens would be forlorn for a time in a new environment, but surely if we're nice to them, they will settle down?

Summer

"Where are they now?"

Michael is just about to answer but the kittens save him the trouble by tearing into the room in a mad game of chase-leap-attack-counterattack-chase-leap-etc. Brown Kitten registers my presence but I don't think the black kitten notices I'm there until I bend down to pat her. The game has started out with Brown Kitten pursuing the black kitten but within a second it's changed tack and Black Kitten is now chasing her. The pair leap onto things, leap over things, scramble under things, dash at each other and, wrestling frantically, roll over and over across the floor.

This is their period of aerial warfare. While watching them I often think that anyone who has seen kittens fight would never have thought of using the term "dog fight" for a World War II air battle (though I guess the prospect of taking part in a "kitty fight" wouldn't have done much for airforce recruitment). And whoever coined the phrase "weak as a kitten" must have had newborn ones in mind, because our kittens abound with energy. Whenever they aren't asleep or washing or eating, they are in perpetual motion: round and round the room, up and down the stairs, on and off the furniture.

The black kitten is the wildest of the duo. At times we have a sense that her hyper-energy even unnerves the brown kitten because now and then I will see one of my kitten fantasies fulfiled: Brown Kitten will be washing Black Kitten's ears. But my imaginary ear-washing had been an affectionate gesture. In real life it's a strategy adopted in desperation. Brown Kitten starts licking the other kitten to stop her tearing round the house at such a speed that all you see is a flash of black.

Despite their constant warfare it's obvious that the kittens are very attached to each other. Sometimes they literally fight each other to exhaustion and stop mid-wrestle to fall asleep with their outstretched paws and feet still touching. At other times they will switch in an instant from chasing each other around the house to curling up together.

One night I go to bed early and am lying on my back reading, when the black kitten comes in. Like most cats of my acquaintance, Black Kitten loves lying on top of people when they're lying on their backs. Within a minute she's stretched out her tiny fluffy body — which somehow manages to be much much longer than you would think when it's fully extended — and is purring blissfully while kneading enthusiastically in the general vicinity of my collarbones. This makes it hard for me to read but Black Kitten is so happy that it seems selfish of me to even think of my own comfort. Also, she's eyeing me lovingly and her purring has reached the volume of a low-flying plane. I put my book aside and simply lie there gazing at this picture of delight.

Then Brown Kitten appears in the doorway. She doesn't do anything. Just glances up at Black Kitten and turns away. The black kitten doesn't look around so she can't have seen Brown Kitten but presumably she can smell her, for without so much as a glance at me, she gets up, leaps off the bed and follows the other kitten out of the room. The whole scene — Brown Kitten entering the room, both kittens exiting — only takes a couple of seconds. When I report this incident to him, Michael says sagely of Black Kitten, "She knows what she has to do."

Summer

The affection between the kittens is all the more conspicuous because as they grow, the differences between them become even more striking. Robin said at the outset that what she and Ron wanted in the new cats was Norton's combination of cuddliness and intelligence. What's unnerving is how completely this goal has been achieved through a near perfect division of the essential criteria between the two kittens.

Brown Kitten is bright and brave and curious. Within a day of her arrival she's gone exploring: out the dining room windows at the rear of the house, across the flat laundry roof, down the fence and into the backyard. When there's an unfamiliar noise — the blender grinding in the kitchen, the fax machine beeping — she immediately looks around to see what's happening. She inspects Michael's computer, monitors our movements, sits on the verandah and surveys the neighbourhood. But she is emotionally reserved. At the start she accepts our caresses but doesn't seek them out unless she wants to be fed, in which case she will start rubbing her head against an available hand or winding her sleek velvety body around our legs in the classic feline figure-eight.

Black Kitten, by contrast, seems to have been born just to be beautiful and affectionate. Ron has told us that when he's working, she'll come into his office every half hour or so for a cuddle and she does the same with us. However, it's soon apparent that she doesn't clutter up her day with mental activity. Michael and I eventually conclude that in the sweetest way imaginable, Black Kitten is the least intelligent cat we have ever met. Even our late Pusscat, who was generally regarded as living proof of the principle that if you've got a lot going for you in front of your ears, you don't need much between them, could be observed having the occasional thought.

It's true that this process was painful to watch. Pusscat would come to a complete halt. Sit down. Assume a harried expression reminiscent of someone in a crisis trying to remember where they've put their keys. And we could see her saying worriedly to herself: "I do something now. Oh yes, that's it — I *think*!"

As we get to know her better, though, it does emerge that there is one thing about which Black Kitten is *very* intelligent, and that's food. Along with her million-dollar eyes and her glamourous black fur coat, she is a gourmet cat. Also, for a cat with no observable attention span she is amazingly systematic about eating. Give both kittens half a grilled chicken wing and Brown Kitten will chew away enthusiastically at hers while the black kitten settles down to contemplate her piece as if it's a fascinating puzzle. Joints are disassembled, each ligament or bit of gristle is identified and eaten in order, and even when both kittens are still only a few months old it's immediately apparent who has eaten which bone because the black kitten's is always cleaner, as if she has managed to gnaw an extra layer off it.

One night I watch her while she investigates a marrowbone. She eats all the meat and gristle off the sides and then from either end. But she must have been able to smell some marrow deep inside the bone and knows there is still more food to be had. Yet no matter how many times she moves the bone around, no matter how many times she turns it over, she can't work out how to get to that marrow. Finally she sits down and stares solemnly at the bone with her big yellow eyes, clearly regarding this situation as a major malfunctioning of the universe.

Also, unlike the brown kitten, the black kitten's not agile. She jumps and leaps as part of their play but at times it looks dangerously as though she has no sense of balance. I first become aware of this one night when I'm going to sleep and hear a thump. I've been aware of Black Kitten at the bottom of the bed giving herself a few last-minute licks before settling down for the night. After half a minute my sleepy brain puts her and the thump together.

"Did she fall off the bed?" I ask Michael.

"Mmm," he says, unsurprised. As he is in the house all day with them, he has had more opportunities to observe the kittens. It's already apparent to him that Brown Kitten has exceptional climbing and leaping skills while Black Kitten clearly needs a refresher course in "Basic Kitten Skills Unit 101: Sitting On Cushions Without Falling Off". But, it has to be said that when the black kitten actually gets herself securely stationed on her cushion, she stops the traffic. Visitors ooh and aah and, as Ron comments when he rings from LA to hear about the duo's progress, you get the impression that she's perfectly happy to spend all her time being petted and admired. Brown Kitten, by contrast, wants to explore the world.

Despite their differences, though, the kittens have one thing in common. Before they left their respective mothers, they had obviously both been taught one rule: "Never let a human being enter a kitchen alone." Ron and Robin have trained them to associate the sound of a spoon being banged against the top of a tin with food. But this skill must have become redundant within hours of being learnt because — without any training at all — both kittens immediately connect the sound of a fridge door opening with eating. Also, it becomes apparent that they could hear a fridge door opening at six hundred paces, through four cement walls, while in a deep coma.

Soon, entering the kitchen becomes a trip into the paranormal. As soon as you go there, you know you are not alone. If you look around instantly — even before the impulse to look around has formed fully in your mind — you will find two small pairs of eyes gazing up at you. They weren't there a millisecond ago. They weren't anywhere around a millisecond ago. But they are here now and the fact — which we always seem to be pointing out to them — that they already have food in their dishes doesn't deter them. You are opening a fridge and the kittens are convinced that you are not allowed to do this without them being present.

THE ACADEMY

When we start telling people about our cat-sharing arrangement, I expect them to raise concerns about the kittens' welfare. Ron, Robin, Michael and I spend so much time worrying about whether the kittens will be upset by moving house that I assume other people will think the same. What I discover, though, is that everyone else is more concerned about it from the human point of view.

"How will you feel," friends say with concerned expressions and premonitions of very nasty custody cases, "when Ron and Robin return and the kittens go back to them?"

The first time I'm asked, I answer bluntly, "Relieved."

It's now February, the hottest and most humid month of the year. On these still, steamy days, any strong odours that develop in the house can build to an awesome extent. As Robin so rightly observed, it's a very short trip from the kittens' mouths to their bottoms. Considering their tiny size, they're gargantuan shitters, and Brown Kitten in particular produces a shit with a stench so powerful I'm convinced that it could have a role in national defence.

"They could take you off in a military jet each morning," I explain to her as she and Black Kitten are hanging around while I'm changing their litter tray one evening, "put you down on some isolated stretch of coast, have you do your bit for your country and fly you back in time for your midday nap."

I'm sure that one of Brown Kitten's shits could deter boatloads of drug dealers and other undesirables from even thinking about landing along thousands of miles of otherwise undefended coast. Indeed, I can see everything going well with the project until the inevitable day when we get the call from the top man who explains to us that the military don't think they can get their own people out in time.

"They'd be worried they could get overcome by the smell," I tell Brown Kitten who's watching me with big, intelligent eyes as if she understands everything I'm saying, "even though they'd be wearing sealed suits and carrying oxygen."

When I'm finished changing the tray, I go into the kitchen, open every window as wide as I can and pour myself a glass of wine. I know exactly what's going to happen next. Brown Kitten and Black Kitten believe in demonstrating their appreciation of our efforts and showing a cooperative attitude towards management. So the instant their tray is emptied they both immediately leap in and produce the largest shits of which they're capable.

Summer

A couple of weeks later when a friend raises the question again, I can't be so glib. I reiterate the advantages of the cat co-owning relationship. Two abandoned kittens now have a home, two homes in fact, and four caring people to look after them while the four of us get to have cats. But I'm glad my friend doesn't press the issue even if her face does indicate she's expecting us to end up as a news item ("Friends in Court over Kittens") because I'm aware this isn't really an adequate answer. It's obvious to me by now that I've bonded with the kittens.

This is a gradual process. It starts with Black Kitten when I'm letting myself into the house one evening and realise she has been waiting in the hall for me to come home. With Brown Kitten, it begins when I discover she does interpretative dancing. She shimmies on her spine around the carpeted curve of a stair with her eyes fixed upon me as I watch her and an expression of rapture on her face. It's shortly after this that I find a name for her.

Well, to be accurate, I find a new name because both kittens have actually got names. The matter of the cats' names is the only area of conflict between us and the co-owners. My clear recollection of our original agreement with Ron and Robin was that I got to name the cats. However no one else, including Michael, seemed to remember this and, to my surprise, when the kittens first came to visit us, they had been christened: "Gladys is the brown kitten and Olive's the black one," Robin said. "We call her Ollie."

As can happen when you meet two new people at the same time, Michael and I got the names muddled up and started thinking of the brown kitten as Olive and the black

37

kitten as Gladys until a couple of days later when the mistake was corrected. But somehow the names didn't take, we only ever used them in conversations with Robin and Ron. At our place they are "Black Kitten" and "Brown Kitten" until I see Brown Kitten doing her spine dancing and decide she shouldn't be called "Gladys". She is most definitely a "Grace". It suits her so perfectly that Michael and I immediately start calling her Grace and I tell myself that Ron and Robin are bound to agree when they return.

The next stage of bonding happens when I drop a carton of milk which spills just as the phone begins to ring. I pick up the carton, go to answer the phone and then come back to mop up the spill. Except that the milk has now formed a neat little lake on either side of which is a kitten energetically licking its way towards the centre with that combination of intensity and contentment only a cat can display.

After that, there's the time I spray a stain on the carpet with some foam cleaner and come back a few minutes later to find Grace and Black Kitten on guard and staring appaled as the foam expands. Their attitude suggests they're prepared to defend the household against every manner of enemy. Except they have never, in all their combined inexperience, envisaged an enemy which doesn't move, doesn't make a sound, just grows and grows before their horrified gaze. I vanquish the monster by rubbing it into the carpet with a brush and they go away, very relieved.

The final stage happens one evening when I come home from work to find Michael sitting on the sofa, engrossed in a phone call. The two kittens are sitting

Summer

beside him. Grace is sitting upright, as she usually does, with her sleek head in the air while the black kitten's hunched down in her fur beside her. I don't say anything, I can see Michael's having an important conversation, but I linger in the room. I'm surprised by the kittens. Usually a new arrival excites them. They jump up and do a few whirligigs around the room. At first I think they must be tired. But then I notice they are looking bright-eyed and alert, as if they're aware of the seriousness of the occasion. They know this isn't a time for play. They are paying attention. I suddenly perceive that I'm the one who's been regarding these two little newcomers as visitors, outsiders, essentially Ron and Robin's cats. That's not the way they see things. When I approach them, they raise their chins towards me with looks that say, "Yes, we'd like a pat but keep it brief, will you, please? We're very busy here, you know. We are helping Michael. Oh yes, it's an important part of what we do. We're the household cats."

After this moment it never occurs to me to withdraw from the joint cat-caring relationship. I know that Ron and Robin are devoted to the cats so it's impossible to consider sole ownership. But at the same time I can't imagine not being involved with the kittens even if there are going to be long periods when I don't see them.

This doesn't stop me worrying about them, though, as the time approaches for them to return to their other home. I am particularly concerned about the black kitten. Even though there's only ten days or so between them, she seems much younger than Grace and I worry that she will be confused and frightened when she goes back to Ron and Robin's. A week before they're due to return, she starts to sleep in a padded cat basket that belonged to Pusscat and I encourage this, thinking that it will give her one familiar object in the other household.

One day I reflect that the apprehensions I'm feeling must be similar to those of parents sending children off to boarding school for the first time and I realise that the whole cat-sharing arrangement in a way rather resembles having kids go away to school. And who better to provide for two young cats in need of an education than Ron and Robin with all their knowledge and expertise? Within a short time my imagination has come up with the perfect boarding school for the kittens and I'm cheerfully telling people that at the end of February, Grace and Black Kitten will be resuming their education at a specialist establishment designed to develop their very different talents and capacities: Ron and Robin's Academy for Smart and Decorative Cats.

I soon find myself mentally composing letters to Professors Ron and Robin about appropriate courses of study for the kittens in their upcoming semester at the Academy. The black kitten, it's obvious, really needs to repeat the entire "Essential Skills for Kittens" course. Just doing the "Not Falling Off Cushions" segment again isn't going to be enough. This is a cat who clearly hasn't got her mind around gravity. Grace, meanwhile, needs to learn how to climb down from places to which she's climbed up. Or alternatively not to climb up to places from which she can't climb down.

However, neither of the kittens needs to do any of the Academy's elective study units on torture. This summer, for the first time in my life, I find myself feeling

Summer

compassion towards cockroaches. The kittens don't eat the roaches that fly in our windows but they love chasing them and capturing them and killing them and dismembering them and they particularly enjoy the phase between the capture and the kill. As a duo they are most effective torturers. Anyone who's ever wondered which form of pain would be worse — pain inflicted at predictable intervals or randomly inflicted pain — would be suitably horrified by the sight of the kittens with a cockroach, because they achieve a synthesis of both.

Grace approaches the matter scientifically. She observes the reactions of the cockroach. She rolls it over on its back and then rolls it the right way up. She watches how fast it can run and puts out a well-timed paw to thwart its escape. Black Kitten's MO is quite the opposite. Her attention wanders. She'll pounce on the cockroach and then get distracted by a flicker of sunlight on the floor. She'll leave the scene for a minute and then come back and swipe the cockroach with her paw just after Grace has set it back on its feet again and the poor insect is fancying it might still have a chance of escape. Michael argues that all this is according to nature and we should not intervene. But when he's not around I carry out a mercy killing as soon as I see Grace and Black Kitten gathering about their prey.

At the same time I've become aware that both kittens urgently need to do a course on dealing with other cats. When they arrive at our place in mid-January they are still babies, and the issue of their relations with other members of their species doesn't seem a priority. By the end of their stay six weeks later, they are visibly growing up and one morning it becomes obvious that they've been leading sheltered lives at both their homes and have no real idea of the existence of other cats.

The first cat they meet — or, to be accurate, fail to meet — is called Naomi. She's an Abyssinian who lives a few houses up the street. She arrived in the neighbourhood as a kitten the previous spring and occasionally I'd see her leaping through the big trees at the rear of the house. I tried to make friends with her but she wasn't interested in contact with unknown human beings. She was a fearless climber and all she wanted to do was explore the trees. When GB came to live next door, there must have been some sort of territorial standoff because Naomi no longer came swinging through our backyard and for the next few weeks we rarely saw her. But we often heard her. She had a penchant for climbing roofs and getting stuck, so that we became familiar with the sound of her wails until she finally learnt the vital lesson about climbing down from places the same way you've climbed up.

With GB's departure, Naomi must have started venturing into the surrounding backyards again. On this late February morning I find her sitting on the fence as I'm going down to the laundry where we have locked the kittens while some work is being done in the house. In the couple of months since I've seen her, she's grown a great deal and is now very definitely a cat. Maturity, though, doesn't seem to be making her happy. I remember her as a beautiful kitten with a triangular face. But her face has now grown long and narrow, and all that getting stuck on the roof and wailing seems to have brought out a depressive element in her personality because her expression is doleful.

Summer

I first think of waving her away before I let the kittens out but I am curious to see what will happen, so I open the door and call to Grace and the black kitten, who are curled up together on a chair. When the kittens appear in the doorway, Naomi's reaction is immediate. Her back arches, her fur rises, she starts to growl and spit. Her yellow eyes morph with rage and her tail starts scything around with such speed and viciousness it looks like it could slice off heads.

I am so startled by her performance that for a few seconds I just stare at her, forgetting the kittens. When I remember and turn to them, it becomes clear I needn't have worried. Neither Grace nor Black Kitten has realised what's happening. Grace is gazing in Naomi's general direction with a look of polite interest. The black kitten hasn't noticed she's there. Naomi is displaying every characteristic of feline aggression with such enthusiasm that I suspect this is her first opportunity, as a newly grown-up cat, to do her routine. I feel embarrassed for her. It's not just that she's completely misjudged the dangerousness of the kittens. Her enemy isn't even aware of her existence.

Ron and Robin return one rainy day at the end of the month and appear around noon to collect the kittens. Grace and Black Kitten have just settled down for their late morning sleep and can't understand what these people are doing, suddenly appearing in the house, exclaiming and talking excitedly.

"They've grown. Look how much they've grown!"

"She's lost that startled kitten look," says Ron, smiling at the black kitten. Then he exclaims, "No, she hasn't. Look — there it is!"

In the evening I ring to ask how they're settling in. I'm most worried about Black Kitten.

"They're both fine and she seems happy," Ron reports. He explains that they'd let the kittens out of the carrier in the bedroom where they had talked to them and petted them for a bit before allowing them out into the rest of the house. "When she went out into the hall and onto the stairs, she stopped for a minute, looking very nervous and then she just ran off down the stairs as if she was saying, 'I remember this place!'"

AUTUMN

AKAs

Black Kitten got her name at the start of autumn. It all began when Michael and I went to dinner at Ron and Robin's one evening in late March. The kittens had been back with them for about three weeks. It's my first experience of being a non-custodial cat co-owner and in the car on the way to their house, I give a lot of thought to being properly behaved. Or, at least, to appearing to be properly behaved. I can give the kittens a pat in passing, I say to myself, but I mustn't get preoccupied by them. I'm here as a guest for dinner *not* to visit them. In any case, they won't remember who we are.

I have the scene neatly laid out in advance in my mind. Kitten or kittens approach or pass by Thea's chair. Thea glances down briefly, only imperceptibly withdrawing from the conversation in progress. Thea strokes kitten or kittens. Kitten or kittens proceeds/proceed on with its/their own activities. Thea resumes

Autumn

full participation in conversation on un-cat-related topics.

What I didn't realise when constructing this scenario is that in using terms like "approach" and "pass by", I was thinking more of aeroplanes than kittens. At this stage of their lives Grace and Black Kitten don't do either. When we arrive they are tearing around the house. Robin explains that they are generally quieter than they used to be but every evening they have a mad hour and regress completely to their hyperactive fruit-bats-on-speed phase. If they come near my chair at all, it's either to charge under it or to race around the back of it. Any time they get near enough for me to think of making an overture, they promptly change course and skitter off in a new direction.

I catch enough of Grace in short bursts over a ten minute period to see that she has grown but is otherwise precisely as I remember her: alert, bright-eyed and big-eared. Black Kitten, though, keeps disappearing under the furniture before I can get a good look at her so I eventually abandon my pretence of restraint and follow her into the dining room where I squat down and wait for her to emerge from under the table. When she finally does, I stare in astonishment.

"What *have* you been feeding her?"

The black kitten has acquired a tail. I have no clear memory of her previous tail and neither does anyone else. It was just small and black. The sort of small black tail you would expect a small black kitten to have. But this one is unforgettable. It's nearly two-thirds the size of her body and in addition to being much too large, it looks heavy. She also carries it awkwardly which, when you think about it, is what any of us would do if we were to wake up one morning and find that we now had attached to our rear ends an appendage nearly as big as the rest of us.

Ron and Robin's view is that the vet from whom they got the cats hasn't been properly forthcoming about the black kitten's antecedents and there is a squirrel somewhere in the family tree. But this is clearly wishful thinking. Black kitten's new tail has none of the perky elegance of a squirrel's: it's sausage-shaped and it doesn't curl. What's buried back there in her gene pool is quite obviously a skunk.

As I am to discover in the coming months, the kittens don't develop in proportion. Eventually, outstanding features such as Grace's ears and the black kitten's tail, while remaining conspicuous, grow more into scale with the rest of their bodies. Before this happens, though, I become aware of the special distinction of Black Kitten's tail. When I see her lying down it suddenly becomes apparent that this isn't a tail, like other cats' tails, meant for communication and carrying about. Black Kitten's tail is designed to transform her surroundings.

It is the unexpected, and perfect, final embellishment of her beauty. With this new addition, her black feathery fur looks more spectacular and serves to enhance every colour and texture with which she comes into contact. When she spreads herself out across a nondescript stretch of buff-coloured carpet, she suddenly becomes a cat in an advertisement. You can almost hear the copywriter's prose. The carpet is classic, contemporary, luxurious and hard-wearing all at once. Homemakers will be queuing to buy it. All Black Kitten has to do is lie down on any surface,

Autumn

open her golden eyes, gaze serenely and her whole life becomes a photo opportunity.

In more practical terms, though, what the black kitten's new acquisition means is a multiplication of the amount of space she takes up and an exponential increase in the amount of fur she manages to disperse around herself. After the kittens return to us in April, I'm coming downstairs with a heavy tray when I notice, firstly, that the previously clean stairwell carpet is now tufted with patches of black. Secondly, and more inconveniently, the black kitten has stationed herself upon a stair to ambush me and because of that huge tail, there is nowhere for me to put my foot.

At this time Michael and I are constantly anxious about doing either ourselves or the kittens a serious injury on the stairs. They have an unnerving habit of tearing down ahead of us and then abruptly slowing down or coming to a sudden halt. Until we get used to this, we're constantly treading on them. One evening when I tell Michael that I've just stepped on Grace's paw, he says he hopes it wasn't the same paw that he has just stood on. After comparing notes we think of ringing the RSPCA and outing ourselves as serial abusers.

"Move!" I now instruct the kitten who is spread across the stair like a black feather boa. "Move!" But she merely rolls over on her back so I can rub her tummy. There's so much black fur both on the stair before me and scattered round the immediate neighbourhood that it really looks as if someone has delivered it by the bucketful. "You are just a fluff bucket!" I tell her in exasperation. Black Kitten gazes up at me happily. Ambushing me on the stairs is one of her favourite pastimes and she clearly thinks I enjoy it as much as she does.

After that I start calling her "Fluffbucket" from which the "The Fluffer" soon gets extracted. This in turn leads to the development of "fluffing" as a verb and to conversations in which one of us says to the other, "Where's the Fluffer? What's the Fluffer been doing?" To which the other replies, "Oh, just fluffing about." In contrast to Grace, who is always observing and exploring and investigating, "fluffing" seems to sum up perfectly the black kitten's activities, which are quiet, unadventurous, don't seem to have much purpose, and involve lots of fur.

A couple of days later, though, Michael does say, "This might not be a good idea."

I know what he means. My attempts to convince Ron and Robin that Gladys should be renamed Grace were a complete failure. As far as the co-owners are concerned, Gladys is her name. A compromise is agreed on. Grace is her AKA on our side of the city. When the four of us are together, Michael and I try to remember to call her Gladys.

If the switch from Gladys to Grace was unacceptable, I should have realised from the outset there was no hope of converting the co-owners to a new name for Olive, but it seemed to fit her so perfectly that Michael and I are soon using it without a second thought.

But Michael says worriedly, "Robin might think it sounds derogatory."

"But it isn't," I say firmly. I think it signals her extraordinariness. It suits her to have a name that is like a title. She is the Fluffer.

Whether Ron and Robin are astonished or appaled, by

Autumn

Olive's change of name I never discover. There's already a precedent in place and both households adhere to it so that both cats now have akas on the other side of the city. Looking back I can see that coming up with our own names for them was probably an essential part of bonding with the kittens and identifying the need for it is probably the only contribution I can make to the yet-to-be-developed field of cat co-ownership.

At the same time, though, nobody takes the matter very seriously. The guiding principle in our relationship with Grace and the Fluffer is their best interests and, in my view at least, it doesn't concern the cats what we call them. I have in mind the example of our late Pusscat, who not only acquired several names in her years of living on our street but also got her gender and body image altered radically with the result that one set of neighbours referred to her as "your little silver cat" while another woman spoke of her as "your big, fat cat, George". (I thought at first that this woman had gotten confused and was talking about some other cat, but one day she saw me in the street with Pusscat who was small and quite slender and did not look at all like a male. "Hello George," the woman announced. I was half expecting her to tell me that it was time 'George' lost some weight.)

When Grace and the Fluffer come back to us in April, after five weeks in their other home, Michael as usual worries that the break has been too long. "We should have had them over for a few days so they could remember the place," he says.

I answer that I have worked in welfare services and can't help feeling that the kittens are doing very well — they have four devoted adults hovering concernedly over them. Few human children are so lucky.

"Last time," I point out, "when I was so worried about how the Fluffer would cope with going back to Ron and Robin's, she settled down immediately."

I've been more concerned about practical matters like whether the kittens are now aware of the existence of other cats. But Ron has reassured me on this point, saying that they know about other cats and they are suitably wary of them. I agree with Michael that things will be difficult for Grace and the Fluffer for the first couple of days but say I'm sure they will settle down.

In fact only Grace appears forlorn. It's soon apparent that the Fluffer simply lets events wash over her. She loves Grace, cuddles, people, eating and playing. How things work and why things happen are matters of no interest to her. As a result perhaps, she's the first cat I've ever met who doesn't display moral outrage and never gives us those hurt, astonished stares, those how-can-you-do-this-to-me! looks which cats are usually so good at.

It's obvious that all this is very intellectually frustrating for Grace but it turns out that the Fluffer is capable of making her own observations. One night when I'm worriedly watching Grace, who's sitting up on a pile of telephone books in the corner of Michael's office and looking unhappy, I see the Fluffer, who's been drowsing contentedly on the office sofa, give her a glance and then look at me. The look says simply, "She gets fraught."

I can't help but nod. Fraughtness is exactly what Grace's manner is conveying. She's obviously trying to make sense of what has happened to her. How she's been in one house with one set of people and the Fluffer. And now she's in *another* house with *another* set of people and the Fluffer. Everyone is being very nice to her. *But it's not the same.* And while she has nothing to complain about, she doesn't understand what's going on and she's not happy.

I have a sudden sense of what we'd be faced with if Grace was human. I can see her as one of those precocious teenagers who create a scandal and make themselves instant celebrities either by writing a sexy novel or penning their candid memoirs. This idea's no sooner occurred to me than I find myself visualising exactly what book she would write. It would be called *Fraught*, and it would be a scathing indictment of how she and her adoptive sister were raised by agreement between two sets of parents. Both couples want to have children, but without sacrificing their careers and lifestyles, so they settle on this joint arrangement. Naturally they don't inform the adoption authorities of their plans and one couple are the official parents. From their earliest days the children move from one house to the other and think of both places as "home". It isn't until they get to school that they begin to realise how unusual their situation is. But by then they're so bonded to both couples, they can't conceive of making a choice even if they were to be given the opportunity.

It's easy to see what would happen once Grace's book gets published. This would be a whole new angle in the genre of brilliant-talented-young-person-with-tormented-childhood books. She'd be on every television talk show and social commentators who had been spending years worrying about the effects of single parenting would now be able to turn their attentions to the new and equally vexatious subject of quadruple parenting. Proponents could praise it as a significant social breakthrough in view of overpopulation while critics could dismiss it as a cold-hearted, destructive experiment by a group of self-indulgent careerists. Either way I figure Grace would be onto a winner. I could see her being on top of bestsellers lists and generally being the hottest new celebrity.

While I'm contemplating her literary career, Grace gets off the pile of telephone books and takes herself across the room to join the Fluffer on the sofa. Both cats conduct an extensive laundry exercise and a detailed examination of their undercarriages and then curl up together for the night. Grace pillows her head on the Fluffer's new and expanded tail. She has a very practical attitude towards this recent arrival which she treats like a cross between an accessory and some new form of soft furnishing. She can often be found asleep with her chin comfortably burrowed into it or with it wrapped around her neck and shoulders like a shawl. The Fluffer never seems to mind.

THE CAT'S WHISKERS

It's still early but already getting dark when I come home from work one evening and hear a kitten crying. Grace and the Fluffer aren't in the house. Alarmed, I open the dining room windows to call them. "They're okay," says Michael, coming into the room behind me. "It's another cat." I lean out and see that the kittens are sitting at the edge of the flat laundry roof. They are peering down at a third little cat who is perched on the garden fence below them and crying her heart out.

I assume she's a local cat who's become lost. There are no breaks in the row of terraces that line the street and occasionally wandering cats get caught behind the continuous wall of houses and try to get home by going through a strange house.

When I call the kittens in, the lost cat follows and in the light from the windows, I see a perfectly shaped little tabby face that's a whole series of upward and downward curves. She has markings in black, grey and ginger; large, black-outlined greenish eyes that tilt upwards at the corners; and a pretty, dark mouth and nose. But what most impresses me are her long white whiskers which sweep out and down and then curve inwards to almost meet under her chin. They remind me of depictions of cats in Chinese paintings while simultaneously making me wonder about evolutionary purposes. I can't see why any cat needs whiskers so elegant they look as if she gets them styled each morning at some high-priced salon.

"Well," I say as she approaches me, "aren't you the one!" And fall in love.

The little tabby is very distressed. She stares up pleadingly at Michael and me and when I reach out to stroke her, she rubs her chin desperately along my hand. The kittens go off to eat their dinner while Michael and I inspect her. Neither of us has seen her before. She's young, we guess a couple of months older than the kittens, and we decide that she's new to the area and probably from one of the houses across the back lane. Perhaps Grace, on one of her expeditions around the neighbourhood, has passed through this not-quite-grown cat's backyard and the little tabby has followed her across the lane and up along our side fence and now can't work out how to get home again. We think that once our kittens are no longer outside to distract her, she'll find her own way back.

But an hour later when we come downstairs again to eat, she's still sitting on the garden fence. Also, the next door neighbours have become concerned by her crying. We can hear them talking, worried there's a cat trapped somewhere. As I open the windows though, there's a

Autumn

sudden change of tone. A torch has been trained on the edge of the laundry roof where Grace and the Fluffer, attracted by the noise and the clamour, have perched themselves and a female voice is cooing, "Oh, pretty kitty — look at her beautiful eyes." We realise that while the kittens have been with us frequently during the past few months, our immediate neighbours have never seen the Fluffer before, and now they're completely diverted from the plight of the crying kitten by the sight of her posed in her glamourous black fur and gazing down benignly at them with her million-dollar eyes.

Hearing us open the windows reminds the kittens of the important things in life and they come hurrying inside to check their food dishes. After a minute the lost cat follows them. She jumps up from the fence to the laundry roof and tentatively crosses the roof towards us. I give her a pat, and she immediately starts to purr and curve her chin around my hand. I say to Michael, "I think she's hungry too — can't we give her anything?" We place a dish of milk and some dry food on the laundry roof. She eats it all quickly, glancing up at me constantly between mouthfuls.

I watch her and start to worry. She's in good condition but her manner is very intense — she's plainly eager to come inside. She looks to me like the sort of cat who'd be too fixated on her owners and her usual surroundings to ever think of wandering away from home. My guess is that her sense of adventure is about as well developed as that of the Fluffer, and the Fluffer would no more take the short trip across the back lane on her own than I would cross the Himalayas on foot. I am suddenly sure she hasn't strayed or become lost.

"She's been dumped."

Michael agrees. We decide that the real test will be whether she remains overnight.

When we come down in the morning she's sitting on the laundry roof, peering in the dining room windows, plainly waiting for us to appear.

"Isn't she pretty!" I exclaim as I feed her. Michael is less impressed. He thinks the new cat is undistinguished. She isn't gorgeous like the Fluffer or intelligent like Grace, nor is she a cat with style and presence like GB. She is just a straight up and down regular moggy.

"And," he adds, "she whines."

I agree that the new little cat does cry a lot, which neither of the kittens do. Grace makes an occasional chirp-chirp noise which I assume is some sort of modified Burmese cry. It sounds nothing like a meow and surprises me every time I hear it because I feel that such a bright and elegant cat should have a more impressive voice. The Fluffer, by contrast, has a beautiful, soft, deep, musical voice but at this stage of her life she rarely uses it except to give little murmurs when we arrive home and neglect to notice her curled up in a ball next to the umbrella stand, waiting to welcome us.

The only occasion while she's a kitten that either of us ever hears the Fluffer do a serious meow is once when she inadvertently gets locked out the front door. For the Fluffer, whose idea of adventure is to sit on the windowsill above the heater and watch the outside world through the glass, a quarter of an hour on the street on her own is a desperate business. Hearing a loud, deep, unfamiliar meow outside the front door, Michael goes to investigate

Autumn

expecting to see a large, strange cat. Instead there's the Fluffer, very eager to come in. (When he tells me this story I immediately go and embrace the Fluffer. "Fancy knowing your own house," I say to her proudly, ignoring the fact that by now Grace can effortlessly navigate her way around most of the suburb. Any signs of normal competence are always welcome in the Fluffer and I get as thrilled by her displaying some perfectly ordinary feline skill as I would if I discovered that Grace had her own Web site.)

The new cat, by contrast, has a frequent high-pitched cry and she meows in a tone that seems to call for a reply. It's not a "let me in" or "feed me" cry but a constant series of complaints and grievances: "Where have you been? What have you been doing? I've been waiting for ages, I thought you weren't coming."

Michael zeroes in on this. "And she's always wanting attention," he says. "GB and the kittens have a lot of social assurance."

"She's been dumped," I point out, "GB and the kittens have had gilded lives. Her whininess will settle down once she feels secure."

"She wants someone to love her," says Michael, who can see what's coming. He turns to the new cat: "You know how to spot a sucker."

He's right on both counts and I could never claim afterwards that I wasn't warned, right at the outset, what she-who-gets-to-be-Kate is like.

I put some breakfast out on the roof for the new little cat. Once she's eaten, she moves up closer to the windows. The kittens sit on the windowsill watching her. She peers past them into the room and then looks at me, obviously seeking permission to come in. I'm in a chair at the end of the dining table hovering over the morning's paper. She glances at the kittens and I can see her thinking, pair of spoilt, petted, don't-know-what-real-life-means, rich bitch princesses.

Then she turns back to me. When our eyes meet, her look says — plain as day — "Get rid of these two and I'll be your cat."

"Actually," I find myself replying silently, "they'll be leaving in a few days."

It's the last week of April, Ron and Robin are due to return to Sydney the end of the month. Since GB's departure I've never thought of getting another cat, but here's this lost, lonely little individual, clearly in need of a home. She can be our permanent cat and we will have the kittens on visits. I can't persuade Michael to like her as much as I do but he is willing to adopt her. I find his criticisms simply make me like her more. I agree she's an utterly ordinary moggy — not especially bright or adventurous or beautiful — but I'm going through that stage of infatuation when even the adored one's least impressive characteristics turn out to be exactly what you want. I say to Michael, "We've got one cat who thinks she's human and one cat who thinks she's a feather boa. A cat who thinks she's a cat suits me fine."

We christen her Kate. I think it suits her. She is definitely not the sort of cat to whom you would give an exotic or romantic name, although for a short time I do consider following the fashion of the street and calling her after a great historical figure (we have a Mozart and an Einstein

Autumn

in the neighbourhood). But in her case, this means a great woman and somehow the great women of history didn't get named suitably for my purposes. If I call her by their first names, the point will get lost as nobody will realise that Joan relates to Joan of Arc , Emily to Emily Bronte or Christabel to the Pankhursts.

At the same time the surnames are awkward. "Wollstonecraft" is clearly too long a name for any cat. (Just try going outside and calling, "Wollstonecraft, Wollstonecraft, Wollstonecraft," unless you've got the breath control of an opera singer.) And I can see it being shortened to "Woollie" just as "Pankhurst" would give way to "Panky". Bronte and Austen are possibilities except that "Bronte" has become popular for soap opera heroines while "Austen" sounds like a man's name and will probably lead to complications at the vet's.

Michael and I decide we'll keep on feeding Kate outside for the next few days until the kittens return to Ron and Robin's. This will also give us time to find out if she's really been abandoned or has just decided to relocate from some other household in the area. (Our experience with Pusscat, who would finish her specially cooked supper of lightly grilled chicken wing and then go out and convince some gullible new neighbour that she was completely unloved and neglected, has made us deeply respectful of the thespian talents of cats.) Kate will be allowed to come in during the day, but will continue to sleep outside at night.

We also see this half in/half out period as a way of trying to limit conflict, because tension is already building between Kate and the kittens. She often sits on the laundry roof close to the window while the Fluffer sits inside on the windowsill and they paw at each other. Grace doesn't fight but watches warily. Michael says she is morally outraged at my championing of the new cat and indeed one morning when I'm putting a bowl of milk out for the newcomer, Grace peers at the bowl as it passes over her head and then looks straight up at me as if to say, "What about *us*?"

Things become more complicated when Ron's job is extended and his and Robin's return gets delayed until the middle of May. Kate continues to sleep outside and we are sure she's getting fed at other houses because sometimes she turns up at our house, licking her mouth and looking conspicuously uninterested in whatever we have put out for her next meal. But she's still very keen on moving in. Whatever her story is, wherever she's lived before, she knows all about the perks and privileges that pertain to being a resident cat. She's had midday sleeps on comfortable chairs in sunny rooms. She's dozed in the evenings in front of televisions. She's spent nights curled up at the bottom of beds. She's had it all before and she wants it all again. When she appears each morning at the window, she looks to me for approval and then, with a wary glance at the other two cats, comes in and seats herself on the nearest available chair for a wash and a sleep. But her real intention is to move further into the house, and Grace knows it.

Fights start erupting between the two of them. There are skirmishes in the hall and up and down the stairs. Grace usually wins the battles and Kate becomes more circumspect but then Grace starts coming in to sleep with

Autumn

us. In the past it has always been the Fluffer who liked to appropriate part of a pillow or curl up in the curve of a body, but now Grace appears as we're settling down for the night. She arranges herself in a neat ball at a bottom corner of the bed, directly opposite the door, and it's obvious that her presence has nothing to do with company, warmth and affection. This is territorial. Kate is being kept out.

SHE-WHO-WAS-KATE

In the late autumn afternoons, Grace starts to take journeys. She has always been adventurous, she's climbed all the surrounding trees and explored every neighbour's backyard, but now she begins to disappear for hours. The first time it happens, Michael gets anxious and leaves his desk every five minutes to check if she's returned. But after a few days we stop worrying. She always comes home in time for dinner. In addition to all the exercise she's getting, she's having a growth spurt and food's a priority.

I'm by the window one evening when she returns and I watch her as she picks her way along the fence and across the roof. She halts briefly to swoop her head, droit du seigneur style, into Kate's food bowl to finish up the remaining scraps before coming in the window. It's obvious immediately that she's travelled a great distance. Her long slender legs are so tired they can scarcely support

Autumn

her. She has to sink down in a chair and rest before she can take part in the evening round of feeding, washing and reinforcing the pecking order with Kate and the Fluffer.

At the same time she begins to have a social life. She has visitors — Mozart, a smart black tom kitten from down the street, and another cat, a Burmese whose name we never discover but whom we call the "green cat" because she's a shade of brown that's moving towards a moss tone. These two are around the same age, give or take a couple of months, as our cats. They're utterly uninterested in Kate and the Fluffer and also completely dismissive of Naomi, who by now has also become a frequent visitor. Initially they come to collect Grace to go out and play but after a week or so, the socialising and the games become centred in our backyard and, to our astonishment, we suddenly discover we are the hottest spot in the neighbourhood for the under twelve-months-old feline set.

As soon as a couple of cats start visiting regularly, the curiosity of other cats in the area gets roused. Pretty soon we notice we're having even more visitors. Cats are clearly on their mobiles telling other cats about our place. Strange cats of all ages come wandering along the fence at all hours of the day just to peer into our yard and see what's going down. There aren't any fights between the residents and the visitors. Kate and the Fluffer merely sit and watch the new arrivals, who in turn seem scarcely to register their existence. Grace meanwhile appears to take it all for granted, as though she's always known she was going to be a leader of cat society.

She is so clearly the top cat in the household that we think the apprehensiveness she shows at night when she sits on the end of the bed, alertly watching the door, ready to repel Kate, is an overreaction. Also, while Grace is swanning round with the smart cat set and being lauded as the season's hottest hostess, Kate — who's some months her senior — spends her days in the kitten-like activity of chasing wine corks across the kitchen floor. (One of the first things we notice about Kate is that in some ways she's clearly had a deprived childhood because she's enthralled by champagne corks. By this time Grace and the Fluffer have reached the point where they wouldn't deign to play with one unless the champagne is French, vintage, and totally out of our price range.)

In addition, when Kate and Grace fight, Grace still usually wins. Kate primes herself for the attack and then tears fiercely towards Grace. But at the last moment, just before Kate launches her assault, Grace turns her head, casually sweeps out a paw and swats her. Kate retreats. Michael frets about the fighting but I'm more sanguine. I'm convinced that once Kate feels secure, she'll settle. I'm sure that boundaries will eventually be agreed on. She can't go on fighting forever. It must be apparent to her that an accommodation has to be reached.

Already there's been some signs of truce. One day I stay in bed with a cold and, after her breakfast and morning walk, Grace comes back into our room to survey the situation. The weather is wet and chilly and she clearly thinks it would be a waste of resources for me to occupy the warm bed on my own so she resumes her position by my feet. An hour later the Fluffer quietly sidles in and eases herself first onto my pillow and then into the narrow gap between the top of my head and the wall which, as usual, soon leads to her

Autumn

appropriating the entire pillow. Finally Kate appears. Grace opens a wary eye as she leaps tentatively onto the bed and stands there plainly anxious to join the party. I pat the mattress beside my hip and she moves forward and settles down. Lying there in a bed festooned with cats I'm very aware of them all being totally conscious of each other's presence while affecting utter ignorance. "You are actresses," I say to them. "You're all actresses."

The serious trouble, when it comes, is not between Kate and Grace but Kate and the Fluffer. I go away for a conference for a few days. When I return, all the cats are having one of their major sleeps — the two o'clock doze which follows on from the midday siesta and precedes the three o'clock wash which then sets them up properly to gain the full benefit of their late afternoon sleeps. (Anyone who claims that cats do nothing all day but sleep obviously doesn't realise what a demanding, intensive and highly systematised activity this is.) They accept a pat, purr, and continue with their sleeps — except for the Fluffer, who escorts me upstairs where she shimmies up and down on the hall carpet in her pleasure at seeing me again, twisting and curving on her back to show her general delight and excitement.

"You are the sweetest cat," I say, immediately forgetting delays at the airport, exasperation at not being able to get a taxi, and fatigue from late nights and sleeping in unfamiliar beds.

When I arrive home from work a couple of days later, Michael is looking grim. He says he has found the Fluffer hiding under our bed. "Kate's turned on her lately," he explains. "While you were away I had to shut her out sometimes. She can't get rid of Grace, so she's taken to attacking the Fluffer. The Fluffer is trying to do her territorial thing, but she's no match for Kate. And Kate's sneaky. She behaves when you're around but she's got a nasty streak. I noticed the other day that the Fluffer was acting oddly but it wasn't until this afternoon that I realised what was wrong. She's terrified."

I sit down and we look at each other. Unlike Grace, the Fluffer appeared to accept Kate's arrival as just another event that life's served up to her. She seemed to realise that she couldn't compete with either of the other cats and didn't try to do so. In fact, of course, she doesn't need to. Most of the time she has no trouble getting what she wants. Most visitors fall in love with her the first time they see her and she responds just as warmly: "Let me gaze up at you adoringly with my big yellow eyes and purr rapturously" seems to be her standard response to the human race. Soon after Kate's arrival, I could imagine her looking at the other two cats and concluding philosophically, I guess I'm at the bottom of the pecking order. But, oh well, I'm pretty.

The thought of the poor Fluffer holed up under our bed, alone and frightened, upsets me. I immediately feel guilty. I've been careless. I should have seen this coming. I know Kate is ruthless, I should have realised she would soon start attacking the Fluffer. Even though I make excuses for Kate, I can see she's a fierce personality. There've been times lately when she's reminded me of those thriller movies in which the new nanny/neighbour/flatmate turns out to be a psychopath

Autumn

who's intent on killing off the hero/heroine and taking over their lovers, lives and offspring.

I can't get the picture out of my mind of Kate stalking the Fluffer. I can see Kate waiting for Grace to go out and then pacing around the house and finding the Fluffer in all her curling-up places and leaping on her. Physically the Fluffer is as strong as the other cats, if not stronger, but this only gives her a temporary advantage because she doesn't seem to focus long enough to win her fights. We have watched her and Grace wrestling since they were tiny. The Fluffer will use her strong front legs to pin Grace to the ground and will be standing over her and then something happens. Mostly it's an event we can't detect. An interesting smell has wafted by or some little insect has appeared. In any case the Fluffer's attention shifts. When she turns back to Grace it's with a mild preoccupied expression, more like somebody resuming their knitting than an adversary going in for the kill. I know that the Fluffer can fight Kate but I can see she wouldn't be able to cope with Kate's relentlessness. Kate would find it easy to intimidate her. I realise what we must do.

"We'll divorce Kate."

Michael looks at me as I continue firmly, "Other people have been feeding her and she's a pretty cat — even if you don't think so. Some other house will take her in. We've got to protect the Fluffer, she's our first responsibility. It's a good thing this happened now while it's still early in the piece. We'll just stop Kate coming in."

This is relatively easy to do because Kate has never discovered how to get into the house through a kitchen side window that is fixed open. Grace and the Fluffer only use this window when the dining room windows and the side hall door are closed. Even then, they mostly use it as an exit and prefer to wait around until we let them back in because getting in the kitchen window involves a big leap up from the side path onto a narrow ledge.

When Kate reappears that evening, her food is left out for her on the roof as usual. But the main windows are kept shut. I pretend to be oblivious to her staring at me through the glass and reaching up to scratch at the wood so I'll open the windows. All I can think about is the poor Fluffer, trembling under the bed.

Finally I look at her. "It's not going to work out," I tell her. "Go away. There's a lot of cat-friendly households around here. Go and find yourself a house *without a cat.*"

I know, of course, that we should take Kate to the vet's or to the RSPCA as an abandoned pet. But I feel that most households would prefer to adopt a small kitten rather than a nearly-grown cat and I know what happens to cats when homes can't be found for them. Kate talked her way into our house in twenty-four hours. Other neighbours are already feeding her. I figure her chances of finding new owners through her own efforts are better than through official channels.

I'm convinced that we're doing the right thing and once Kate is exiled, the Fluffer becomes noticeably happier. I find I can't sit and eat at the dining table in the evenings because Kate gazes sadly at me through the windows. However, that's easily managed. For the next few nights we have dinner in front of the television and I learn to walk through the kitchen with my head at an angle so I can't see her big eyes watching me and her mouth opening in

Autumn

unheard yearning meows. When I speak of her I say firmly, "She-Who-Was-Kate."

I find this difficult but I tell myself it must be done. After a couple of days her vigil ceases. She still comes by from time to time but then we notice that the food we put out for her hasn't been eaten and we don't see her at all. I tell myself it's all for the best. Three cats are obviously too many cats, even if two of them are part time. It wouldn't have worked out.

VIOLINS AND SNOW IN THE STREETS

A couple of days later, Ron and Robin return. We tell them the story of Kate and her expulsion and Ron nods and murmurs something about Kate learning tough behaviour out on the streets. Afterwards, though, there's something about their quiet response that makes us feel we've overreacted. As Michael says to me later, the kittens are still not fully grown. Also, the Fluffer's both the youngest and the slowest developer. Perhaps at the time of their next visit, when she's a couple of months older, she will be better able to cope with Kate. Grace and the Fluffer leave with Ron and Robin on Saturday morning. Over dinner at a restaurant on Sunday night we decide we've been hasty and if Kate hasn't found another home, we ought to readopt her.

Autumn

It's around ten when we return home and I immediately go to the windows and call her. Outside everything's still and quiet. It's a coming-onto-winter Sunday night in the suburbs, everyone is indoors watching television. I keep calling Kate, confident that in a couple of minutes she'll come running along the back fence, but nothing happens. Then I remember that she likes an early bedtime. I guess she's got in somewhere for the night, as I blow a kiss to her, wherever she is, and go to bed myself, looking forward to the morning.

But the morning's a repeat of the previous night. There's no response to my calls, no movements in the trees that could suggest a cautious cat watching our yard and no neighbours leaning from windows to enquire, "Are you looking for the little brown and black tabby?"

I start doing worried estimations. We began excluding her about nine days previously. And we haven't seen her for four days. Perhaps another house has taken her in. Maybe she's left the neighbourhood. Or she's been injured. Been taken to the vet. Been discovered to be homeless, and is now dead. I go off to work thinking that if she doesn't reappear tonight then she's definitely gone.

That evening it's cold and we are both late home. I call out to Kate but again there's no sign of her. Thinking that the smell might attract her we put some fresh food out on the laundry roof and then we sit and eat our dinner at the dining table before the windows, hoping that she will see us. Michael's sure she's left but I'm still optimistic. It's only nine days. I keep thinking of all the times during those first three or four days when I turned away from her unhappy face as she stood meowing at the windows.

The Cat Who Looked at the Sky

She finally appears when I've almost given up. Michael is loading the dishwasher and I'm finishing my coffee when I decide to try one last time. I call to her and hear a faint answering cry.

She comes across the roof very slowly and stops at the windowsill. I immediately feel guilty. I can remember an evening, just two weeks earlier, when we had guests for dinner and she appeared at the windows. Seeing that neither of the other cats was about, she strolled in cockily. Purring loudly and eyeing off the guests, she picked her way along the windowsill until she reached my side, whereupon she rubbed her head up and down beside my cheek in a proprietorial manner. Tonight she's an entirely different cat. She seems frightened and she approaches the bowl of food we've put out for her warily.

We realise things have been tough for her these last cold nights. "I think she's been chased," says Michael, surveying her, "and she's been hiding away somewhere."

She doesn't look well. The uptilted eyes are puffy, and her coat when I reach out to touch her feels cold and oily. The brash invading princess of two weeks ago has completely disappeared. After she's eaten, I have to coax her to come inside and to sit upon a chair that I've drawn up for her between me and the window. She lets me stroke her but she doesn't reach out to rub her chin along my hand as she always used to, and she doesn't start to purr. We begin to worry that she's sick. Michael brings a rug and wraps it round her. She finally consents to sit down on her haunches but is still very watchful, obviously expecting this interval of warmth and kindness to be brief. Whatever's been happening, she no longer has any

Autumn

illusions about her welcome anywhere. She's braced for things to start turning ugly. "It's alright, Kate," I keep saying, stroking her gently and trying to be soothing. "It's alright."

Now that the other two cats are no longer around for comparison, it strikes us both how young she is. She's probably not even fully grown yet and already she's been abandoned by one household and exiled by another. We wonder that we could ever have been so harsh to her. We agree that she should be taken to the vet, perhaps she has an infection. With Michael in attendance on the pair of us, I pick her up, wrapped in her rug as though she's an invalid daughter, and carry her upstairs to the sitting room where the heater's been turned up in readiness. I sit down carefully in an armchair, tuck the rug around her again and stroke her gently. I'm beginning to feel like I'm in a Victorian melodrama.

After a while Kate breathes a sort of sigh as if she's given up. She's tired and it's all too complicated for her to try and work out what's going on. She stretches out a paw across my knee, settles herself into a more comfortable position on my lap, and goes to sleep. My experience of cats suggests to me that somewhere in this saga of reunion and restoration she must also have staged a full-scale wash with her legs arched over her neck and each ear earnestly and industriously rubbed. But if she did, I don't recall it. I just remember thinking that all that was missing from this scene was the violins and the snow in the streets.

If Kate had been a proper Victorian heroine, she would have died happily in my arms that night, knowing that at last she was loved and had found her true home and, what was more, had tripled sales for that clever Mr Dickens. As it is she sleeps all night on a chair in the dining room and is described by Michael early the next morning as looking surprised but happy, clearly unable to believe her good luck. Three days later she gives the impression of having been resident cat all her life.

Within three days, too, she also looks perfectly healthy. Indeed, even next morning it's apparent that her peaky appearance was probably due to fear and misery rather anything physiological because she's eating and playing contentedly even though she gives us a look every now and again as though she is not sure it's all really happening.

I decide we ought to allow her a week's grace before putting her through the ordeal of a visit to the vet. "Let's give her time to settle in," I say. I'm secretly afraid that her previous owners might have had her microchipped with a computerised identity tag, although this seems unlikely if she's been abandoned. "She's had a tough time this last month, a lot of shocks and changes, she ought to have some time now just to enjoy herself as resident cat."

The first evening we readopt her we decide that we'll just handle any toilet crises that occur. We were never sure what happened in the past when she was visiting but she'd never made any messes in the house. Next morning we put her nose to the gap in the kitchen side window and she immediately understands its purpose. She leaps from Michael's arms, exits, presumably inspects her territory and does whatever else she needs to do, and then promptly returns the same way.

Autumn

For the first time in his acquaintance with Kate, Michael is impressed. We know the kittens are younger than she is, but when we taught them about the side window, it took even Grace a day or two to grasp the concept (the first time she came back in of her own accord, she pranced into Michael's office to show him what a clever cat she was). The Fluffer was much slower. Weeks later, she could still sometimes be seen on the side path staring up at the window with a look of consternation on her face while she slowly turned the matter over in her mind: I'm outside. I want to be inside. I think I can get inside by jumping up onto that ledge. Then I walk along the ledge to the open window. Then I bend down and go in the open window. And I'm inside again. At least, I think that's how I can get inside again.

It soon becomes apparent that Kate has thoroughly developed ideas of what is due to a resident cat and one of the things she expects is full 24-hour, 360-degree access to us. We already knew that she wanted to sleep with us at night and we soon get accustomed to her wishing to be constantly around us. But we're startled to discover she doesn't like us using the bathroom without due surveillance. Unlike many cats, she isn't frightened of running water. Instead she watches the shower with interest and is positively fascinated by the sight of water swirling down the plughole.

In fact she doesn't seem afraid of anything that can happen in the bathroom except being left out of it. The bathroom door has swelled slightly in Sydney's monsoonal summers and doesn't close completely unless we remember to apply full pressure. Within a couple of days she discovers she can open it by hurling herself against it so it rebounds and we become used to her careful scrutiny while we carry out every facet of the morning's toilet routine. My theory about this behaviour is that her previous owners were kidnapped by a spaceship while they were taking a bath, hence her anxiety. Michael says he wouldn't be at all surprised in tones that imply he thinks there are a number of things about Kate that need explaining, and from what he's observed of her so far, alien abductions could figure prominently in all of them.

She soon establishes her daily routine: a session of voyeurism in the bathroom followed by as much breakfast as she can extract from the pair of us through a mixture of pleading, seduction and outright fraud, followed by the morning's instalment of her favourite pastime which we soon christen the Great Paddington Solo Cork Chasing Marathon. Then there's a whole series of short and long washes and long and short sleeps until late afternoon when there's a further instalment of the Marathon and assorted other running, chasing and being-demented-underfoot-type activities followed by dinner and a contented sleep on a human lap in front of the television and/or a foray around the neighbourhood prior to bed.

If Kate has any recollections that her kingdom was once shared with two other cats, she seems to have deleted all memories of this. Or perhaps when she smells traces of Grace and the Fluffer about the house, she just decides that their disappearance and her restoration were all part

Autumn

of the same glorious but inexplicable event. At the time we take her back in we don't expect to see Grace and the Fluffer for a couple of months but less than a fortnight later, the duo come to visit again for a week while some excavations are being done as part of renovations to Ron and Robin's house.

We decide to try and keep the cats apart as much as possible. Our first priority is to protect the Fluffer while trying not to upset Kate too much, but the week goes very quietly. The time span between visits has been so short that the three cats return to their early relationship. Grace immediately reinstates herself as top cat while Kate sometimes raises big hurt eyes towards us but mostly seems resigned to the situation. It's as though she's decided she was having this wonderful dream where she was sole resident cat but now she's woken up. There's some hissing and scrapping and Kate refuses to eat near the other two, but no major conflicts occur and she doesn't harass the Fluffer. The first night Grace occupies the end of our bed as if she's never been away while the Fluffer curls up in one of her usual spots in the corner of the upstairs landing and Kate sleeps on her favourite chair in the dining room.

At the end of the week, Ron and Robin come to dinner one evening and take Grace and the Fluffer home with them while Kate's asleep. In the morning she paces around the house obviously wondering where they are and that night she ignores the opportunity to join us in the bedroom. Instead she curls up in the Fluffer's corner on the landing, burrowing down into the carpet as if covering herself in the Fluffer's odour will either bring

The Cat Who Looked at the Sky

back the missing cats back or prevent her from disappearing in the same way. The next morning she appears to have forgotten their existence

WINTER

BIKER TOMS

As winter settles in, I'm aware that I'm postponing Kate's inaugural trip to the vet. I have plenty of rationalisations: the weather's wet and windy, I haven't gotten around to buying a pet carrier and, after all, it's only been a month and anyone can see she's a perfectly healthy and happy cat. A bit demanding perhaps, but I feel this is understandable given the circumstances and not something I can expect a vet to fix. So I let things drift until a crisis occurs.

Early one morning, seeing her stretched out on her favourite chair, I give her a stroke in passing as usual, but instead of opening her eyes in sleepy acknowledgment, she swings around and glares at me and gives a cry. I look at her in surprise — Kate usually likes being petted. At first I think I've startled her but it's such a fierce reaction that I go and make some coffee and then come back to her. I talk to her quietly for a minute and then repeat the caress

Winter

to watch her response. It becomes clear she doesn't mind me touching her head but running my fingers along her spine upsets her. I go upstairs to consult Michael, thinking she's had a fall. No — been swiped by a car, that would be it. Maybe she's been bruised. Has broken ribs, internal bleeding. In keeping with the universal law that crises always happen on wet weekends, it's a Sunday and it's raining. We make an appointment with the vet for the evening and set off to buy a carrier.

By this time Kate has abandoned her chair and is out in the back garden. When we return with the pet carrier, we hear the sounds of a wrangle. We open the windows to see her scampering up the fence towards us pursued by a large black and white tom. She hurtles into the protection of the house and the tom stares after her from the edge of the roof. I've never seen him before and am relieved I haven't.

Forget about cats you wouldn't want to meet late at night in a dark alley, this is a cat you'd feel nervous meeting at midday on the main road when you had an armed escort. He's a thug biker tom with a broad chunky build and ears that have been through so many fights they've become fringed around the edges. But the most ominous thing about him is the way his face is patched. Whole teams of Hollywood experts have clearly been at work for months on the design of his face, and come up with a truly frightening arrangement of patch and eye in which each eye seems to peer out at you from a patch of black at an unexpected point, with the result that you don't feel you're looking at the same pair of eyes but at two unrelated spots of evil.

The Cat Who Looked at the Sky

By early afternoon I realise that whatever it was that has hit Kate, it wasn't vehicular. She stays indoors and seems to be having a normal enough day of alternating sleeps and washes, except that her manner is agitated and she starts to wriggle, belly-down, across the cork floor in a way we've never seen her do before. It's obvious to me now that she's on heat. I suppose I should have realised this much earlier, but all my serial cats had been desexed and while I'd grown up on a farm, where it's commonly assumed that children know all about animals and learn the facts of life as a matter of course, this didn't apply to me. Also, I must admit that when it comes to sex, I've never quite understood how children were supposed to achieve these feats of lateral thinking. I never saw a cow or a horse using the telephone or catching the school bus, so it simply didn't cross my mind that we reproduced in a similar fashion. It's true this was partly a matter of personality. I was a dreamy child who got captivated by the unusual and faraway. At thirteen I'm sure I knew more about the Principality of Liechtenstein than I did about the operation of our farm, although what I knew about Liechtenstein was, because of the vintage of the books in our local library, at least twenty years out of date (if that matters in Liechtenstein's case).

But it's also true that there wasn't a lot going on for me to observe. My parents had both come from large poor Irish Catholic families in which I suspect the rate of reproduction was in inverse proportion to the number of times the topic was mentioned, and it seems to me now that our animals must have been brought up in the same tradition. Calves, foals, pups and kittens invariably arrived during the night and, for all the evidence I ever saw to the contrary, were reproduced by immaculate conception.

I overheard things, of course. But this didn't help much because the terms used on the farm in relation to sex were either so vague, or so archaic, as to be completely misleading. I can remember, for example, asking once what a "heifer" was and being told it was a young cow who had not been with a bull. At the time this made sense. There were only one or two bulls on the property and they were kept in paddocks far away from the heifers. It seemed to me quite reasonable that so far their paths hadn't crossed. Unsurprisingly, it was a while before I realised that "springing heifers" were not young cows of exceptionally athletic disposition but young cows about to have their first calves.

During the afternoon the rain gets heavier and Kate stays indoors, but the thug biker tom doesn't leave. He sits under a tree at the end of the backyard and after a time he begins a series of meows so piteous that I keep going to the window thinking it can't be him, some other cat must have arrived. But yes, it really is him, Mr Cat-You-Never-Want-To-See-Again, who's sitting down there and issuing this haunted lonesome sound which clearly says in cat-to-cat language: "Yeah, babe, I know people think I'm a real mean guy. But believe me, darlin', underneath this tough facade, I've got a loyal 'n' lovin' 'n' sensitive heart."

That evening as Kate emerges hesitantly from the dimness of her pet carrier onto the examination bench in the brightly lit surgery, Emma, the vet, exclaims, "Oh, isn't she pretty!"

A few minutes later she tells us that Kate is not

microchipped, has never been desexed and is now coming onto heat which explains her sensitivity about being touched on her lower spine. She is also younger than we'd thought, maybe only six weeks older than Grace and the Fluffer. But I must confess that I pay relatively little attention to what Emma's saying because I'm too busy thinking about her opinion of Kate's looks. Michael has always been so unimpressed by Kate's appearance that I'm thrilled by Emma's praise.

This must have been obvious because in the car on the way home Michael teases me, saying that my face lit up when Emma said that Kate was pretty. It's a relief he can't read my thoughts because I keep going over the compliment in my mind. One minute I'm telling myself, "Don't take it seriously, vets probably always praise the looks of their new patients — I'll bet they're advised to do so in their professional training." (I could see a lecture hall full of vet science students and a professor intoning: "Always praise the appearance of even the most ugly pet. Remember, a gratified owner is a relaxed owner and a relaxed owner helps relax the pet.") But the next minute I'm thinking, she was genuine. She thinks Kate's pretty. It was completely spontaneous. Nobody could be that good an actress. After that I reflect that Emma likes cats, she probably thinks all cats are pretty. But then I think, she was sincere! She just came out with it. She really meant it! (The debate about Kate's looks finally gets settled to my satisfaction on a later visit to the vet's when two of the other female staff also admire her. "She's a chickie kitty," I announce authoritatively to Michael when I get home. "Women think she's pretty.")

Winter

By the next morning Kate has a number of suitors. Some weeks previously there'd been an article in a Sydney newspaper in which a cat protection body raised concerns about the effects that the large-scale desexing of domestic cats could have upon the feline gene pool. According to this organisation, the increasing numbers of owners getting their pets desexed before they reproduce means that the only cats who do have kittens are either the tiny minority with pedigrees or the much larger bunch of backstreet-living ferals, the dregs of society who never get spayed. As a consequence the cat organisation feared that the agreeable, home-loving, affectionate characteristics of the domestic moggy could be swamped by the feral genes of the antisocial, unaffectionate denizens of the back streets.

At the time I was reading the article I had the Fluffer purring rapturously by my feet while Kate and Grace slept tranquilly nearby in the sun. Considering that all three of them were unplanned pregnancies, abandoned kittens born in different litters in the last nine months and yet possessed of every affectionate home-loving trait you could want, it didn't seem to me as though the cat organisation's genetic Armageddon was imminent. But now, peering out the back windows at the callers our affectionate home-loving little moggy has attracted, I begin to think that the cat protection body might have a point. It's clear that the Dregs of Society have turned up to visit Kate. Hanging around our backyard are a couple of thug biker toms so tough they make her first suitor look like Fred Astaire.

I do have one hopeful moment when, to my surprise, Mozart, Grace's clever friend from the smart catpack, suddenly appears at the window, looking very preppy in his sleek black coat and red collar among all the biker toms. "Et tu, Mozart?" I say doubtfully. I can't believe that he is, for want of a better word, a contender. But then I reflect that perhaps he's also matured earlier than his owners expected. They think he's just out on the street playing games and here he is, fixing to be a teenage father. I have a momentary fantasy about Kate and Mozart's kittens, all inheriting their dad's easy sociability and impressive brains and their mum's gorgeous whiskers, but then reality intervenes. It isn't just the prospect of what Michael, Ron and Robin will say when our combined cat family multiplies to six or eight. There's a more immediate problem.

"You'd better go home, mate," I tell Mozart. "Even if you are serious, I think you're way out of your league." It's obvious that with all this tough company around, a nicely mannered little tomcat from a double-income, two-car family doesn't stand a chance. Not just of having sex, but of surviving to see the comforts of home again.

A day later normality returns. The biker toms disappear, presumably to visit some other little tabby who's grown up more quickly than her owners anticipated, and Kate's booked in to be desexed.

THE MARCHING SEASON

Midwinter, the renovations to Ron and Robin's house turn into a saga. Jobs that were supposed to have been completed in days begin to take weeks. The weather continues cold and rainy. By July they are living in a couple of rooms and the place is full of builders and dust. The cats are perfectly happy in these conditions — they enjoy the activity. Grace climbs up and down ladders effortlessly and escorts the architect around in a professional manner when he comes to survey developments. Meanwhile the huge excavation that's required to fix the faulty plumbing beneath the house provides the Fluffer with an example she aspires to ever afterwards when it comes to digging her own holes. Michael and I know that Ron is due back in LA later in the month and aren't surprised to get a call from him one night saying the house is becoming unliveable and they would like to go earlier if we wouldn't mind taking the cats.

We agree but we shake our heads at Kate and say, "Sorry darling, you'd better enjoy the next couple of days, the bitch princesses are coming back."

I know that Kate is going to be upset but I tell myself she will settle. The break between visits has only been three weeks and I'm confident that things will proceed pretty much like the previous time.

But the beginnings aren't promising.

The pet carrier appears in the hall. Grace and the Fluffer emerge and sight Kate. "You!"

Kate looks at us in outrage. "Them!"

Michael and I glance at each other apprehensively. "Us?"

The Fluffer is the first to come into contact with Kate and she immediately lies down and rolls onto her back in a display of friendly submissiveness. Kate doesn't attack her but she's displeased and a few minutes later, when the Fluffer has moved away, she sits and eyes her, clearly thinking about opening hostilities.

Then Grace, who's been out the window to re-explore the backyard, comes in. Grace is certainly not going to lie down and roll over for Kate, but her manner's placatory. She offers her nose as if to say, "Oh yes, I know it's your place — I'm just passing through."

But Kate is affronted. She's been sole resident cat. This has been her kingdom. It's all very well for Grace to imply that she's not here by choice. The fact is: she is here and so is this black cat and Kate wants them both gone. If, as seems to be the case, Michael and I are not going to remove them, then Kate will do it herself.

Serious fighting breaks out that first evening as the cats

wait for their dinner. Kate chases the Fluffer up the stairs and then turns on Grace, who runs into Michael's office and leaps onto a pile of telephone books in the far corner. There are more skirmishes when the Fluffer returns downstairs but I'm relieved to see that the additional weeks of growing up have made a difference to the Fluffer. She doesn't seek out fights but she can defend herself and will counterattack, fiercely and successfully, if Kate pursues her.

The Fluffer, also, seems delighted to see us again. She immediately resettles herself in all her favourite places — by the skirting board in the hall outside our bedroom, on my pillow when she's in the bedroom, on the lid of the linen basket in my study, and on the windowsill in the dining room. It's as though she's never been away.

The real change that's occurred is in Grace. We expect her to just take up her position as top cat again, as she did during her brief return just a few weeks before, but this time everything is very different. Michael says that when the cats arrived, he saw Grace looking around. Her face was set like a truculent teenager's who's obliged to go and stay with dull relatives. Her expression said clearly, "How long have we got to stay here?"

She's soon making it plain that she has no more desire to be with us than Kate has to have her stay. To our surprise she shows no interest in any of her old friends in the smart catpack. In complete contrast to only a month ago when she was running the neighbourhood's most fashionable feline salon in our backyard, she has become solitary. It's as though she's another cat entirely. She no longer even goes on journeys. Instead she sits on the top of the pile of phone books in the corner of Michael's

The Cat Who Looked at the Sky

office. This position is probably adopted for sound defensive reasons but it also strikes us as symbolic. It's the furthest point you can go and still be in the house. It's obvious that she's mourning Ron and Robin.

As far as possible she tries to ignore Kate. She attempts to avoid hostilities but there's no hope of this. I watch one morning as Grace tries to pass Kate in the hall between the kitchen and Michael's office. Kate has just come down the stairs as Grace enters and stops to watch her. Grace goes to the food dish, takes a couple of mouthfuls of food, pauses, sits down, gives a paw a lick. To me everything she does looks overstated in its casualness, as if she's trying to say to Kate, "Hey, I'm just passing through, having a bit of a nibble, washing my paws, no need to get agitated."

But it makes no difference — Kate attacks her. Grace tears into Michael's office and I follow her. Michael and I look at each other. Grace leaps up onto her pile of phone books. Michael gets up from his desk and goes over to give her a pat. She raises her chin to accept his caress. She's a polite cat and wants to make it clear to us that she doesn't dislike us, she just dislikes the situation. We don't blame her. Around this time a visitor to Michael's office surveys the three cats and says admiringly of Grace as she stalks by elegantly on her slender legs. "There goes boss cat."

"Of course I'm boss cat," Grace's expression announces as she gives the visitor a scornful glance. "Why wouldn't I be boss cat? Stuck here with a hysteric and a dummy!"

"She doesn't want to be here," Michael says sadly as he strokes her. Grace is his favourite. He hates seeing her unhappy. I remind myself that Michael usually expects the worst. Between his tendency to expect the worst and mine to feel guilty when anything goes wrong we could, given the right opportunities, double the nation's suicide rate overnight. I tell myself that regrets and grim forebodings aren't going to help the situation.

"She'll settle down," I say firmly.

But privately I'm doubtful. There's a quality to Grace's depression that suggests the world has turned completely against her. When I see her sitting upon her pile of phone books, gazing at me with her large sad eyes, I keep remembering how I'd imagined her as a precocious teenage author who'd penned a bestselling exposé autobiography.

It's obvious what's happened since. The classic too-young-to-handle-fame story. Spent all her time partying with the fast crowd and got addicted to uppers and downers and everything else that was going. The press that was courting her a year ago now compete to publish the most embarrassing pictures and the most scurrilous gossip. She's had to go into a clinic to dry out. She got a notoriously huge advance for her second book, *Fraught and After*, the tell-all account of her life on the celebrity circuit, but the money's all gone and of course she's deeply in debt. Her brain's too addled by chemicals and misery to compose a sentence but her publishers have given her a deadline. So now she's holed up in a cheap motel, heartbroken and trying to write . . .

The atmosphere in the house gets grim. Meal times are the flashpoint. They usually coincide with the main morning and evening news bulletins and while we're in the kitchen cleaning out food dishes and opening tins, we hear reports of fears of violence in Northern Ireland. August is the traditional month for the Protestant apprentices to conduct their commemorative marches and it's expected that fighting will break. There's expectations of fighting breaking out when they attempt to pass through the Catholic areas. We know the feeling. At our house we have a marching season every morning and every night.

It usually begins when Kate comes sweeping down the stairs with her face set and angry and her eyes wide and mad. Half a minute later there's growling and hissing and the sounds of a chase. Looking at Kate one evening as she arrives to do battle with her unwanted visitors, I reflect that Charlotte Bronte would surely recognise that vengeful expression and fixed stare. "Oh damn," I say to Michael, "Mrs Rochester's got out of the attic again."

We end up making a joke of it: "Kate's come down with a fit of the Mrs Rochesters," we observe to each other. We're relieved that arson is beyond her capabilities because self-preservation doesn't seem to enter into her calculations. She constantly loses her fights with the other two cats but she keeps on attacking them. "Give it up, Kate," we say to her constantly. "You can't win." Michael thinks she's neurotic. I think she feels compelled to fight. Perhaps she even thinks she's protecting us. Whatever the explanation, the situation gets very very repetitive.

The only encouraging aspect is that there are quiet periods between the battles. Calm descends in the late morning as the trio settle down for stage one of their siesta and remains in place until late afternoon when war resumes in the run-up to the evening meal. Also, even in the marching hours there'll be moments of quiet. I'll come into the kitchen sometimes to find all three cats sitting tranquilly in a line at roughly equal distances apart. One in the foreground, one in the middle and one in the background, as if they've just invented perspective.

Occasionally too, despite the hostilities, there'll be cooperation. Kate and Grace stalk insects together, and one morning all three of them take an immediate dislike to the new brand of cat food we've bought. They make their feelings plain. "They looked at me like I was a war criminal," reports Michael, in hurt tones. I go to investigate and find them all still gathered around their untouched dishes. The Fluffer has got her "Things are not as they ought to be" expression on her face, which is as far as she goes in reacting to unsatisfactory developments. Grace and Kate, though, are in high moral outrage. It's clear that at no time in the entire history of cat-human relations have cats been treated so badly. I tell them they're totally spoilt but I know when I'm beaten. "Okay, okay," I say to their cross faces, "I'll go and get you something else."

These incidents, though rare, feed my hopes that eventually things will calm down. In the midst of all the warfare I even manage to have fantasies that one day the three will get on so well that we'll find them all curled up together on a chair like my imaginary black and white kittens.

But despite my determination to be positive, I become increasingly worried. Apart from Grace, sitting in sad isolation in the furthest corner of the front office, Michael is also concerned about the Fluffer.

"She's bored," he says. "She's not frightened any more, she just wants out of the place when Kate starts carrying on."

I've also noticed that when the Fluffer sees Kate building to a crescendo, she often quickly goes out the nearest window. I feel sorry for her that the situation has become so bad she has to leave, but then something strikes me. "That's progress," I point out. "Being bored and leaving is considerably better than being intimidated and hiding under the bed."

We try various strategies to reduce the conflicts and to make each cat feel cared for and secure. We agree that we mustn't attempt to discipline Kate when she attacks the other cats. It is clearly not something she can control. Separation seems the best approach so at day's end Kate is often on her own in Michael's office, gazing half in yearning, half in outrage, through the glass door towards the kitchen where the Fluffer will be seated on the window ledge quietly observing dinner preparations. Grace meanwhile will have gone off somewhere. She'll come back later in the evening when the battle front has quietened.

I often remind myself that the most sensible response to what's happening is to keep calm and maintain a sense of humour. But I also feel that because I was the one who wanted to adopt Kate, I'm responsible for the situation and begin to wonder if we should be seeking professional advice. At the same time I can't conceive of anyone telling us anything we don't already know.

As I see it, we have three options — live with the situation while trying to resolve it; give Kate away; or tell

Ron and Robin that we'll have to find someone else to care for Grace and the Fluffer when they're out of the country. The fact that we never even discuss options two and three means that we know they're untenable from the outset. Apart from the problem of finding suitable alternative carers, we want to keep all of the cats even though we often look at them and think, how did we get into this situation? This time last year we just had Pusscat and she seemed enough of a handful. Now we've got three!

MEN WHO FALL
IN LOVE WITH CATS

I tend to read my way out of crises. One day it occurs to me that I could consult cat advice books. As I soon discover, though, the local bookshops seem to specialise in either cat-raising manuals (full of specifications about how to build scratching posts) or books about the inner life of cats which aim to help you access your moggy's soul. In addition to these core interests there are usually a couple of books of cat photographs, cat cartoons and cat anecdotes.

As I'm rapidly scanning the chapter headings and indexes of these various cat advice books, looking for something closer to our situation than guides to souls and scratching posts, I find myself remembering my days as a bookshop assistant. Among the unexpected hazards of the

Winter

job were customers who'd ask for books that didn't exist. In authoritative tones they'd request a title you'd never heard of and couldn't locate in any of the bibliographical guides. Polite inquiries about the author, the publisher or anything else that might help you identify it, would eventually reveal that the customers knew this was the book they wanted, so they'd come in to buy it. The fact that it hadn't been written never seemed to strike them as a problem. As I gaze at book covers featuring funny cats, mystical cats and excessively healthy cats with impeccable muscle tone, I want to ask the invariably polite and helpful shop assistants if they have any copies of a publication which is geared precisely to the needs of our unspiritual and unharmonious but perfectly healthy trio. It bears the title "Managing Warring Cats Who Eat Well".

The next logical stop is the local library. At the start I just intend to borrow books about cat-raising and cat problem-solving but while I'm diligently trying to decide between the various 100-things-you-need-to-know-about-your-cat books, my attention keeps wandering to books about the history of cats and the memoirs by cat lovers. Finally, after a week of systematic library visiting, I end up with a huge pile of books beside my bed and have acquired a lot of new information about cats. I learn, for example, that cats always wash themselves in the same sequence of limbs and body parts — or so some writers claim. (I do wonder if this is true of all breeds of cat but my commitment to research doesn't extend to obsessing Grace, Kate and the Fluffer to see if they all do it in the prescribed manner.) I read so many accounts of the sex lives of cats I could practically write my own DIY guide to going on heat. And I discover a whole new romance genre: Men Who Fall In Love With Cats.

At the same time, though, I realise that I've set out on my reading program with the assumption there is an agreed body of knowledge about cats. This doesn't seem unreasonable. People and cats have been living together for thousands of years and millions of cats currently live with millions of people. I just expected that someone would have gotten the topic under control. Instead I discover that the attitudes and approaches of writers to cats vary widely. After a time I begin to divide my cat experts into three broad groups.

In the first group are what I call the Practicals. The Practicals focus on nutrition and promoting your cat's health. They don't give much consideration to your cat's psychic life but they're very detailed in relation to issues such as grooming — in one book the directions on how to wash your cat make the whole process sound only slightly less complex than installing a new Pope at St Peters.

The next group I call the Sensitives. The Sensitives are everything that the Practicals are not. They are very excited about the uniqueness of cats and while properly concerned with nutrition, exercise and grooming, their real interest is in cat psychology. They are passionate advocates of cats' rights and make it clear that every feline failing is the result of some human error. I am certain they would be outraged by our cat co-owning arrangement and, as usual, I feel anxious and guilty until I'm reassured by the sight of Kate, Grace and the Fluffer contentedly washing themselves after dinner. They don't look as though they're being exposed to unparalleled cruelties.

Winter

The final group I term the Self-reliants. Their position seems to be that modern domestic cats, unlike their wild ancestors, never really mature because being cared for by human beings allows them to remain permanent kittens. A lot of the advice given by the Self-reliants is aimed at encouraging your cat to stand on its own four feet rather than looking to its owner to solve its problems. At first, after an overload of Sensitive experts, I'm impressed by the Self-reliants. I like the idea of encouraging my cats to be independent. But after a while I notice an underlying moralism about them that worries me. Also, as sources of advice on cat raising, the Self-reliants are even more demanding than the Practicals and the Sensitives. I begin to feel that raising the fully mature and well-rounded cat is going to require a huge amount of observing and monitoring and behaviour modification. I can see us ending up running a household that's partly a four star feline resort and partly a cats' reform school.

My attempts to develop a solution to the problem of our warring cats from these differing approaches gets further complicated by my apparent inability to successfully apply even the simplest information I'm acquiring to Grace, Kate and the Fluffer. For example, I try to memorise what moods are, according to various authorities, indicated by what tail positions. (Broadly speaking, tail up equals confident and cheerful and tail down equals glum and anxious). But in practice it doesn't seem to work with our cats.

Grace's tail executes sinuous curves and arches which don't resemble any of the descriptions in the tail-watching literature but do suggest she's trying to communicate with us in Arabic. Kate's tail doesn't tell you anything you couldn't have guessed from one glance at her as she comes into the room. The Fluffer's tail, unsurprisingly perhaps, seems to lead a life of its own. It will be thrashing about in ways that are supposed to indicate divided loyalties, deep ambivalence and ongoing inner turbulence when the little black cat seems to be her usual serene and sweetly unfocused self.

As I'm making my way through the cat books, I can't help but assess what I'm reading as much from a writer's point of view as from that of a concerned cat owner. For example, when I go to the local libraries, I soon notice that there are always many more books about dogs than there are about cats. Usually there are three to four jam-packed shelves of dog books and only one and a half of cat books. I'll be leafing through the cat books when I suddenly discover that stocks have given out and I'm now gazing at guides to raising rabbits. (All the rabbit books seem to focus on the rabbit's early years which puzzles me until I learn that they don't live all that long, so there's not much of a market for books on the older rabbit.) Or alternatively, I'm looking at manuals on raising hamsters; keeping bees; or, my particular favourite, the care of fancy mice. (I soon can't sight the spine of a book on fancy mice without imagining a very flash mouse indeed stepping out of a low-slung foreign car to open the door for an equally cool and soignée-looking lady mouse.)

I know that I shouldn't have been surprised by the discrepancy in numbers between dog and cat books. One of the classic American jokes about writing is that if you want to produce a guaranteed bestseller, you should write a book

Winter

with the tongue-numbing title of "Lincoln's Doctor's Dog". The rationale is that books about President Lincoln always sell, books about doctors always sell and so do books about dogs. So if you can combine all three elements in the title, you're bound to have a winner. Nonetheless, considering that there are almost as many pet cats as there are dogs, I feel, on the grounds of social justice, that libraries could try harder to represent the interests of cat lovers.

As a writer, though, I have a different view. The more I read about cats, the more apparent it becomes that cats are a difficult subject for writers. The essential problem is that they just are. They don't lead action-packed lives that lend themselves to narrative or even to detailed description. Compared to dogs, they're models of unresponsiveness and inactivity. They don't bark when they hear a car start up outside. They don't go and fetch their leads and gaze soulfully at you until you take them for a walk.

One of the books I read is an account of a study conducted at the end of the seventies. The Natural History Unit of the BBC decided to investigate the behaviour of non-domestic or "farm" cats, by which they meant cats who lived in barns but weren't fed by, and had very little contact with, people. A farm was specially hired for the purpose. With appropriate amounts of scientific rigour, a suitable colony of farm cats was identified and relocated to their new home where a researcher was installed to monitor their behaviour. A clear outcome of the study was something that any observant six year old will already have noticed. As one young zoologist wrote, his round-the-clock sessions of cat-watching often revealed "little — except that cats spend a lot of time not doing much".

Under these circumstances I decide that it's not surprising that the bestselling Men Who Fall In Love With Cats books all begin with men who are committed dog lovers and convinced cat haters. Despite their differing ages and nationalities, all of these writers are much the same — they're rather gruff literary characters who spend the first thirty, forty, fifty years of their lives being utterly opposed to cats, hating to ever have a cat in the same room as them, pretending to be allergic to them, scrupulously avoiding contact. Then one day the special cat arrives. It's invariably a kitten. Occasionally, in the time-honoured way, it comes over the fence. Sometimes it's introduced by a cat-loving girlfriend or fiancée who's privately sceptical of the narrator's avowed cat-hatin' position.

Anyway, by the close of day one, the narrator's given the kitten some milk and a tentative pat while maintaining that it will definitely be leaving the next day. But come the dawn on day two, he's in love. With a well-timed purr or a meaningful look, the kitten has overcome his resistance. It's too young to realise he's a cat hater and, of course, his cat-loving girlfriend/fiancée is conniving with it. He keeps saying that the kitten's leaving while getting more and more concerned about its welfare. Finally, he admits he's succumbed.

After that each book follows a similar pattern. Mostly after a month or two each of these kittens has the presence of mind and grasp of narrative principles to go and get itself lost. Bereft, the owner plasters the neighbourhood with posters, knocks on doors, waits up all night, can't believe the kitten's gone for good. And then, just when all hope seems lost, the kitten reappears.

Winter

It's been locked in a cellar, fallen down a mine shaft, got itself shut in an attic. On its return it is skin-and-bones, but it gets well again quickly and starts demonstrating its special skills and charm so that by the end of the book, the owner-narrator is completely converted and the household now usually contains three or four cats.

After reading several of these books I gaze thoughtfully at our three cats and wonder if any of them has the potential to be the heroine of a Men Who Fall In Love With Cats romance. The situation doesn't look promising. The trouble is that these cats who get cat-hatin' men to fall for them all appear to be perfect. A few foibles, perhaps, but usually ones that mimic their owners' sensibilities — they're gourmets, for example, or they've no patience with fools. But mostly they're model animals, universally admired, trophy cats.

And fond as I am of them, it's nonetheless obvious to me that Kate, Grace and the Fluffer are flawed. I have to exclude Kate from consideration at the outset. In all these books the subtext is that the cat is saner than the human being. (The cat teaches the owner about love and life and happiness.) I've never been as dismissive of Kate's sanity as Michael, but I still feel that it's not, perhaps, her strongest point and it would be unreasonable to propose her for a job where it was one of the essential criteria. Despite her charm and sweetness and beauty, I also think that the Fluffer wouldn't make the grade. The cats in these books have to be good at rising to the occasion and the Fluffer expects occasions to rise for her. It wouldn't cross her mind that she had to manage one of the cat-hatin' curmudgeons. In a crisis I think she'd simply go and crawl under a bed and wait for things to get better. Which leaves Grace as the only likely candidate. She's clever, brave and beautiful. A bit nervy, perhaps, but in a very intelligent way. Except that I know exactly what Grace's reaction to the situation would be. She would snap irritably, "It's difficult enough living with people who love cats without being expected to deal with people who can't stand them!"

Given how little real progress I'm making with getting assistance from the cat advice books, it's a great relief when Grace suddenly decides to get over her depression. She stops sitting in her mourning position on the pile of phone books in Michael's office and starts to actively take part in the household. Instead of sidling away from conflicts with Kate, she turns when appropriate and gives her adversary a firm quick swipe. The message is clear. If Grace has to stay, she's going to be top cat.

As part of letting the other two cats know the score, Grace also begins to demonstrate her superior competencies. The most conspicuous of these is her ability to do what we call "alpine walks". An alpine walk consists of an entire tour of Michael's office without touching the ground. Grace begins by jumping up onto the desk in the corner, then walks along the narrow windowsill to the point where she can leap onto the table that holds the answerphone and the fax machine. Then she leaps up to a mantelpiece from which she can jump onto Michael's computer desk. Another jump takes her to the top of the filing cabinets from which she can cross to the second mantelpiece which holds a row of books (she walks on top of the books), then another jump to the sofa followed by a final leap to the long table which holds files and papers and she'll have circumnavigated the room. A further point is that all this above-ground travelling is done without disturbing anything.

Kate always wants to do anything that Grace does. It's at this time that Michael starts dubbing her "Kate the Emulator". I think this makes her sound like a cousin of Ethelred the Unready and queen of somewhere unsuccessful in the Middle Ages. But I can see his point because she's always imitating the other two cats. They have only to adopt some new hidey-hole or take up some new pastime and she'll be desperate to try it. Immediately Grace ceases grieving on top of the phone books, we find Kate sitting there looking very pleased with herself, quite clearly having no idea of the significance of the position.

When Michael sees Kate watching while Grace does one of her alpine walks, he closes his eyes in horror, knowing what's going to happen next. Kate doesn't have Grace's perfect balance. When she jumps she lands heavily and she can't negotiate her way along narrow ledges without either knocking things off or half falling off herself, which then leads to a desperate scramble to regain her footing. It takes several falls and a disproportionate number of casualties before she accepts she can't do an alpine walk. Afterwards, though, her envious eyes always follow Grace whenever she takes one of her above-ground strolls around the office.

While we are delighted that Grace has recovered her joie de vivre, her return to normality doesn't do anything for domestic tensions. We wake to the sound of scuffles in the hall as Kate pursues one or other of her unwanted stepsisters or Grace, in retaliation, chases her. During the marching hours Michael and have only to appear in the kitchen for Kate to feel compelled to attack the Fluffer. One second things will be calm, the next Kate will be hurling herself onto the Fluffer's neck and sinking her teeth in. The Fluffer reacts to these attacks very competently. There'll be a growl and a hiss and the next second, Kate will be spinning over to be held down by the Fluffer's strong front paws.

Despite her proficiency in dealing with Kate, I feel very sorry for the Fluffer having to put up with these constant attacks — until one morning when I see her lying stretched out and relaxed-looking in the kitchen. Kate comes flying towards her. Immediately the Fluffer turns, seizes Kate around the neck with her paws and throws her over and I realise that her position has been a feint. She wanted Kate to think she was off guard, Kate fell for it and, as usual, was defeated. Afterwards I say to Michael, "It's hard to know whom to feel most sorry for. There's Grace who's bored and irritated by the conflict and tries to avoid it. The Fluffer, who can win all the battles but is not aggressive. And Kate who feels compelled to fight but is always getting beaten up."

Meanwhile I keep reading through my bundles of cat advice books. In the time-honoured way I become knowledgeable about matters which are never likely to figure in the lives of my cats, such as new mothers who refuse to nurse, and I develop a great respect for owners of Siamese cats. Indeed, I get the impression that Siamese cats could keep the whole cat advice industry going on their own. The ones I read about seem to spend their entire days contriving new means to make their owners miserable when they come home from work in the evenings.

I also begin to get acquainted with the enormous number of things that can go wrong with cats. I'm always worried about traffic and dogs and, in the Fluffer's case, catnapping. I now go to sleep at night thinking about unfortunate cats who overgroom out of anxiety, cats who refuse to eat, cats who repeatedly run away, and cats who projectile-vomit to convey their distress with their circumstances.

It's actually these accounts of the behaviour of sad and tormented cats that help to resolve our situation for me. I suddenly realise that in addition to observing what is happening, I should also be observing what isn't. It's true that our cats are exhibiting what some writers variously refer to as "meal time conflict" or "meal time stress", but it hasn't occurred to any of them to overgroom, self-mutilate, or express their feelings by regurgitating their dinners. As for leaving home, I can imagine three pairs of eyes widening in astonishment at the idea: "Don't be silly. We live here." Even Grace, the most intelligent and highly wrought of the trio, lacks the obsessiveness necessary for really dramatic displays of unhappiness. In the saddest and darkest of her mourning days, when she was sitting sorrowfully for hours on her pile of phone books, we noticed she was still always first at meals.

THE ARRIVAL
OF GRAVY

Sometime during the winter, without noticing it's happening, we stop talking about "the kittens" and start talking about "the cats". As we are to discover, the trio still have some significant growing up to do, but the disproportions of kittenhood begin to disappear. The growth of the rest of the Fluffer's body catches up with that of her enormous tail and one day I notice that while Grace's ears are still very big, they no longer dominate her face. Previously, I often wondered whether it would be possible to trim a bit off each outsized ear and attach it to the sides of her tiny chin.

Other developments aren't quite so fortunate. Grace has become what people once used to describe kindly as "an enthusiastic eater" and sometimes, after she's been displaying her enthusiasm, there's such a big discrepancy between her little head, skinny legs and football-shaped midriff that it looks as if we ought to hire another part Burmese to walk around ahead of her with a sign saying: "Danger — wide load".

Visitors suggest we put her on a diet. Michael and I nod in agreement and when our formerly svelte Grace walks past us with her belly projecting a good inch wider than her shoulders on either side, we tell her that she's gaining too much weight and something has to be done about it. At the same time, though, we suspect there are two types of cat owners: the owners whose cats eat what they're given, and the owners whose cats dictate what they eat. It's so obvious to me which category we belong to that I'm always amazed when I hear people announce, "My cat eats what he/she's given, or he/she doesn't eat."

My theory about the being-dictated-to and eating-what-you're-given categories is that it depends on the cat. I think that Kate, who's not really interested in food, would consent to an eat-it-or-starve regime, while the Fluffer, who was born a gourmet, would eat enough at home to stay alive. At night however, she'd become one of those elegant and obviously expensive cats you sometimes see on city streets, incongruously but efficiently tearing open garbage bags. As for Grace, she is so completely in charge of her eating arrangements that while Michael and I are telling her she should be on a diet, we are also giving in to her campaign to insert an extra meal into her day.

I don't know where Grace gets the idea that cats are entitled to lunch. My first thought is that she remembers the palmy days of kittenhood when there was always food in her dish. I try to explain: "The reason you always had food then, Grace, was because you didn't eat it all at once."

Now, she not only clears her own plate but usually starts in on the other cats' dishes. Kate and the Fluffer like to have meals in stages. They eat part of their breakfast and then come back later on for another snack. Grace follows a similar pattern but she stays at the food dishes longer and returns at shorter intervals. As we soon notice, this means that she ends up getting the pick of the food.

When we first start buying food for Grace and the Fluffer, I realise that Michael and I aren't used to making decisions about what our cats will eat. During the reign of the late Queen Pusscat, meals were dictated completely by herself. She was relatively flexible about her dinners and would consume chicken wings or carefully chosen selections from our meals or, if neither of these were available, would deign to eat dry food. But she was utterly rigid about breakfast. If we ran out of her favourite tinned food and tried to substitute something like salmon (which she normally regarded as a great treat) she would glare at us in outrage and stalk away from her bowl.

It occured to me, after a while, that I could use this situation to my advantage. Every twelve months or so when Pusscat ingratiated herself so completely into a new household that it looked like she would soon be leaving us, I would try very hard to be gracious to the neighbours who thought she was now moving in with them (which was sometimes difficult — people can be astonishingly patronising when they think they are taking over your cat) but I would also operate on what I called the Rumpelstiltskin principle. In all my thorough going

Winter

discussions of Pusscat's many charms and foibles with her putative new owners, I was careful never to say what she had for breakfast. Much less hint she was so obsessive about the topic that for the first two years she lived with us, she had gone back to her old house at the start of each day to eat. Her previous owners had not revealed the secret to us until they formally ceded her to us when they moved out of the street. Now I did the same. That way I knew that no matter how settled Pusscat appeared to be in her new home, at some point in the morning she would have to come gliding through our kitchen window for her daily fix of pilchards in prawn jelly.

After seven years of being restricted to buying one, and only one, brand of tinned fish, it takes Michael and I some time to start being adventurous about food for the trio. At first we buy whatever's on special or looks most healthy until one day, in an indulgent moment, one or other of us buys a solitary tin of the most expensive brand on the market. This turns out to be such a hit with all three cats that they sit around their empty dishes afterwards, licking their chops, their eyes aglow, their world transformed by a rather unexpected coupling of fish and rabbit described on the can as "field and surf". Even the Fluffer is enthusiastic, although her idea of what's appropriate in tinned cuisine is more along the lines of "heather and feather — prime hand-raised venison and quail from the estate of the Duke of Craighulme". A combination which she would expect, of course, to be served in a jus of ducally raised duck.

We never quite repeat this triumph — on another morning, the same food gets abandoned by all three cats after just a few mouthfuls — but it sets a standard to aspire to and we come home from the supermarket laden down with tins of various proteins in various price ranges. Somewhere in all of this we discover that gravy has taken the cat-food world by storm and that fashionable cats now eat carbohydrates and vegetables with their proteins.

"Turkey with rice and carrots in gravy," I say doubtfully to Grace the first time we purchase one of these, and I offer the tin for her inspection. She purrs eagerly and I reflect it would be more sensible to consult the Fluffer. Grace is not at all discriminating about food. In fact she's a high sodium/high cholesterol fast food junkie and is developing a positive dislike of healthy food like chicken wings and fresh meat.

All the cats turn out to be delighted by the arrival of gravy in their lives but we soon suspect they're not so enthusiastic about vegetables. We notice that they have a hierarchy of food preferences. First they lick the gravy carefully off the solid cubes of food and then, over the course of the next several hours, they return to their food dishes to make their way through the cubes. At the end of the day, though, there are usually some dry, grim-looking pieces remaining and these contain, we are sure, the vegetables.

One drawback of this larger and more appealing choice of menus is that it simply seems to make Grace even more determined to get even more food. From mid-morning until noon, if Michael and I happen to go anywhere near the kitchen, she immediately comes up to us and performs as if she hasn't eaten for a month. It is then that we begin to notice that the fact, so constantly reiterated it

Winter

becomes one word, "You'vegotfoodinyourdish", doesn't have any bearing on her behaviour. Grace wants lunch. Also, she has a strict definition of what constitutes a meal. It's not enough to put out an additional dry food snack for her at breakfast in the hope this will stop her mounting her campaign later in the morning. She has a sense of ritual. A meal has to involve human activity. To be specific, it involves a human being coming into the kitchen, approaching the cupboard or fridge, extracting the food and providing each cat with a portion.

Occasionally there'll be dialogue between exasperated owners and determined cat. Sometimes I'll snap, "You want lunch, Grace? Well, get yourself a job in advertising."

At other times I try and reason with her: "Grace, you've got dry food in your dish. And it's the nice dry food. The stuff in the cupboard is the cheap brand you don't really like. Go and eat what's in the dish."

None of this has any effect. Most days, by one o'clock, I've gone to the cupboard, extracted the dry food and scattered some in three dishes. At the start I would say to myself that I would only put out one portion. One small portion. A scattering of dry food pieces in just one dish. But the light patter of dry food landing in the plastic dishes seems to sound as loud to the cats as a rock concert starting up next door. Within seconds, Kate and the Fluffer will be in the kitchen. While neither of them are as eager to eat as Grace, expressions of indescribable disappointment will cross their faces if they see that only one portion of food has been served.

Although I'm always reminding myself about the dangers of ascribing human emotions to cats, I know that the reason I find it difficult to resist Grace's overtures is because I get uncomfortable when she does her begging routines. At any other time of day it seems to me that she wears a sign saying, "Yes, I'm a cat. But DON'T PRESUME". I'll give Kate and the Fluffer a pat in passing but approaching Grace has always been a serious business. She likes getting petted. In fact she's quite a smooch and will raise her chin for a stroke very willingly. But you're not allowed to pet her when the other cats are around. If she's contentedly having her chin stroked and Kate or the Fluffer walk into the room, she pulls her head away as if nothing has been happening.

Where food's concerned, though, she's shameless. When Michael and I go anywhere near the kitchen she rubs her velvety body around our ankles in passionate figure-eights while gazing up at us with the huge hyper-distressed eyes of heroines in silent movies. The whole performance is so exaggerated that it's impossible to escape the feeling she's privately contemptuous of us and thinks, oh well, here we go again with the old purring-round-and-through-the-legs routine.

I find myself getting irritated and wanting to say, "How about a little subtlety, Grace?", until I remind myself that the figure-eight routine isn't something she's adopted recently — she's been doing figure-eights around our legs ever since her first visit when she was a tiny kitten. Then I remember that she's always had the same mixture of reserve and manipulativeness. She's not only far more intelligent than the other cats, she's much more complicated emotionally. Ron observed of her when she was quite small that she herself sometimes got muddled about her intentions: "She cons herself," he said. "She acts like she's coming up to work you over for food when what she really wants is affection."

The trouble is that I am always reminding myself of things about Grace. I don't go around constantly reviewing my relationships with Kate and the Fluffer in the same way. When they do something new or different I note it and when there's a crisis, I'll think back over their previous behaviour as part of deciding how to respond, but I don't spend my time around them feeling selfconscious as I do with Grace. I've never had such an intelligent, complicated and gifted cat before and I don't feel confident in dealing with her. Also, I'm sure she knows it. She's the only one of the three cats who prefers Michael to me. I'm glad about this — he understandably gets put out when Kate and the Fluffer ignore him and come to me first for attention and caresses — and she's his favourite. He admires her brains and superior skills. He's accustomed to very intelligent cats. But his easier relationship with Grace simply makes me feel more inadequate.

"I don't think I'm cut out for dealing with clever cats, Katie Kate," I tell Kate one morning while she's sitting on my chest of drawers watching me get dressed. The day's initial round of cat wars are over so Kate has stopped being the mad first Mrs Rochester and is following me around while I get ready for work. "I think I'm just a moggy cat person."

Kate responds with a loud satisfied purr. I know she thinks I was very silly getting into this newfangled cat co-owning relationship in the first place. As we are beginning

The Cat Who Looked at the Sky

to discover, Kate is a cat who's totally pre-wired into being a cat. Her performance is so earnest it's as though she's got inside her brain an all-cat synod issuing directives. Learning how to do things by imitating other cats seems to be part of this pre-wiring because, as we have now realised, Kate's not just an emulator, she gives a whole new depth to the concept of a "copycat". (I'd never had occasion to think about the origin of this word before, just assuming it was one of those coinages that come together because the words seem to fit. But now it's obvious it must have been invented by someone familiar with a Kate-type cat.)

Kate's pre-wiring also gives her very rigid expectations. I noted when she first appeared that she seemed to know all about the perks and privileges pertaining to being resident cat and at times now when she stares at me accusingly, I'm sure she's telling me that I've done it all wrong. She knows I'm one of those people who gets adopted by cats. According to the script we both have in our brains, I was supposed to wait for her. One day she was going to arrive over the fence to become my new cat. She did her part and did it all as soon as she could, granted that she'd had to pack a lot of significant life experiences — conception, gestation, getting born, getting weaned, getting abandoned — into the six months between the Pusscat's death and her first appearance in our backyard. All I had to do was wait and Kate can't understand why I didn't. The system had worked perfectly well in the past and there was no reason to think it would fail in the future. Instead, I've ended up with this situation where I have the legitimate resident cat and two resident

Winter

part time usurpers. In her view it's little wonder there is trouble. "You may be right, Katie Kate," I say to her, stretching out a hand so she can rub her chin against it. "You probably are. But it's too late now. The deal is done. We have all got to live with it and make it work."

Making it work is turning out to be more complicated than we anticipated. A combination of unexpected circumstances — problems with Ron and Robin's house renovations and extensions to Ron's project in LA — mean that our original idea of having the cats alternate between the two households on a bimonthly basis has collapsed. By September we are making our arrangements on the run.

The only general principle we can apply is that, wherever possible, we will minimise disruption for the cats. Accordingly Michael and I arrange to go away for a couple of weeks at a time when Robin can come back to oversee the house renovations and look after the trio. Her first plan is to take them to Rozelle with her but then word comes from LA that Ron is worried Kate may be unnerved by the combination of a new carer and a strange house. He thinks she might run away unless both he and Robin are there to look after her so it's agreed that Robin will stay at our place in Paddington.

I'm privately doubtful that it would ever occur to Kate to run away but I'm very pleased that Ron and Robin are prepared to take her interests so seriously. As we set off on our holiday I'm constantly anxious about her. I know she is the problem child, she can be melodramatic and demanding. Robin has only seen her a couple of times and the last time was one night at a dinner during which

Kate rebuffed both her and Ron's advances. Also, I can't help feeling that it's understandable for Robin to be far more interested in seeing Grace and the Fluffer again than in trying to get acquainted with Kate. I have visions of full-scale cat wars as a confused and insecure Kate spends the whole day prowling the house and provoking brawls.

To my surprise, though, Kate seems to take immediately to Robin. This is probably because she observes the welcome Grace gives her. Grace is usually politely distant with visitors. She'll come into the room and survey them as part of the business of keeping an eye on developments in her domain, but she has no interest in them and would certainly never solicit pats or attention. However, the minute Robin walks in the door Grace comes forward immediately, eyes bright, her head raised, her tail up, and rubs herself around Robin's legs in welcome. It's obvious that despite not having seen her for two months, Grace knows exactly who she is. The Fluffer, by contrast, takes fright at the unfamiliar voice, the luggage in the hall and the general excitement and runs upstairs to hide.

As soon as Robin sits down to have a coffee, Kate is at her side, purring and eager to make friends. I'm immensely relieved. I say to Michael that I hope, after starting off so well, Kate can manage to keep up her good behaviour.

"Robin says," Michael reports a couple of days later, following a phone call home, "that there's only been one major skirmish — otherwise there haven't been any fights at all."

"Really?" I say. I'm delighted for a minute, then I start to worry. If the cats don't fight in our absence, is it something we do that encourages them to fight?

"And Kate's sleeping with Robin."

"Really?" I say again. "Well, that's good."

A few days later there's another phone call. "Robin says that Kate is top cat."

That Kate!, I think to myself, I'm sure she put the 'o's in opportunism!

I say to Michael, "I wonder why I worry about her so much. She copes superbly with adversity."

"Yes," he replies dryly. "It's only normal day-to-day life she has problems with."

SPRING

WASH 'N' WRESTLE

The cats' marching season effectively comes to an end with Robin's visit. The two weeks of change in the house seems to have the effect of calming their antagonisms. When Michael and I come back, there are still skirmishes but a lot of the intensity seems to be gone. Michael's sceptical but I'm convinced Kate's finally becoming reconciled to the presence of the other cats and it's agreed that to further encourage the process, she'll go to Rozelle and stay for a couple of weeks with Grace and the Fluffer when Ron and Robin come back.

One evening shortly after our return, the omens for future inter-cat relations start to look very promising indeed. We're finishing dinner when Kate comes in and leaps onto the windowsill where the Fluffer, as usual, has been sitting and watching us eat. By this time the windowsill is seen as the Fluffer's territory. When she's sitting there, both Kate and Grace give her deferential looks when they're passing through, as though asking permission, and neither of them ever attempts to occupy her favourite spot. This evening, though, Kate sits down next to the Fluffer and, while we stare in surprise, starts to wash the black cat's ears. The Fluffer doesn't resist. Indeed, a few minutes later she returns the favour. Michael and I look at each other. "All very cosy," he says.

Ever since she first appeared in our lives, Michael and I have had a fundamental difference of opinion about Kate. He thinks that she is inherently neurotic or, at best, in the overexcitable end of the personality spectrum while I'm convinced that inside my stormy, demanding, passionate Kate there's a calm, reasonable, pleasant cat who'll emerge once she finally feels settled and secure. After the ear-washing episode I begin to think that at long last my sane, peaceable Kate is going to appear. In the following days I often see her and the Fluffer sitting side by side with Kate earnestly playing mum, and I start imagining a happy future where the two of them are fond companions curled up contentedly on chairs together.

But, after a week or so, this happy relationship turns sour. The trouble is that Kate has always been a biter. When Michael and I are petting her, she starts out by rubbing her chin along our hands and then proceeds to licking our fingers and then to sinking her teeth in. We get used to moving our hands away at exactly the point at which we're about to be bitten. The problem is, she now does the same thing to the Fluffer.

She begins by giving the Fluffer's head a thorough wash. Eyebrows, ears, forehead, top of head, back of head, all done with a lot of industry and great attention to detail.

The Cat Who Looked at the Sky

The Fluffer appears to enjoy this because she sits with her head lowered and still. But then Kate gets to the back of the Fluffer's neck where she licks away systematically for a minute and then sinks her teeth in. We never understand why she does this. Does she think there's something about the top of the neck that requires full dental involvement? Or has she convinced herself that the Fluffer's her kitten and she's now intending to pick her up by the scruff of the neck? There's no mistaking the Fluffer's reaction, though. She immediately swings around with a hiss, then rolls over quickly, throwing Kate off and clawing at her as she does so.

The fact that all her ventures in mothering turn acrimonious never seems to deter Kate. A few hours later, Michael and I will see her diligently licking the Fluffer's black head once again, apparently having forgotten the latest wash 'n' wrestle. We look at each other, eyebrows raised, and then look back at the cats, hoping that this time Kate will realise she shouldn't use her teeth, but invariably she does and a second later, she and the Fluffer are having a fight which invariably she loses.

"You're hopeless, Kate," says Michael wearily.

As usual I say that maybe Kate's still getting over a tough childhood, but even I'm becoming doubtful about this explanation. I've noticed that Grace and the Fluffer's essential personalities have altered little since they were kittens. The Fluffer's still loving and serene. When something goes wrong, she will get her "things are not as they ought to be" look. But how things got to be this way and whether they'll get better or worse are matters of no interest to her. After all, one has Grace around for that. If

Spring

the Fluffer is really upset she'll trot in to see me or Michael for reassurance, otherwise she will just have a wash and a sleep, confident that when she wakes up the world will be back to normal.

Grace, meanwhile, is still reserved and highly strung but brave and adventurous. I'm beginning to suspect that Kate hasn't changed much either. Our intense and demanding moggy was probably an intense and demanding kitten and it's around this time that I observe something which seems to confirm this. After months of fighting the Fluffer, Kate suddenly seems to become very attached to her, almost excessively so. The head-washing is just the start of it. She now begins to emulate everything the Fluffer does.

Apart from her passion for gourmet food (which Kate fortunately doesn't seem to notice), one of the Fluffer's most distinguishing traits is her fondness for skirting boards. Day or night, while the other cats sleep far more comfortably on well-padded lounge or dining chairs, you'll find the Fluffer curled up next to the skirting board in the hall near our bedroom. My theory is that the Fluffer got nervous about chairs when she was a little kitten and took a nap one afternoon on the chair that happened to be Grace's current favourite. Grace made her point about this outrage by simply getting onto the chair herself and sitting on top of the Fluffer as if she wasn't there. The Fluffer didn't react but thereafter never sits on a chair until we buy a couple of new ones and she feels confident that neither of the other two cats has some sort of pre-existing claim.

This particular morning as I'm going to our bedroom I come upon Kate curled up in the Fluffer's usual spot by our door. "What are you doing there?" I ask.

The Cat Who Looked at the Sky

A second later the Fluffer herself appears at the top of the stairs. When she sees Kate in her position, she stops and a look that plainly says "Can't I have anything to myself?" comes over her face. She turns and goes away. Kate snuggles back into the carpet, which must have smelt strongly to her of the Fluffer. I suddenly realise what's happening.

"We've all seen this movie, Kate," I tell her. "Don't do it."

It's obvious that in her imagination she's become the other cat.

As I reflect upon all this, it begins to strike me that Kate is probably more calm and flexible about human beings than she is about other cats. Robin and Ron are due back in two months time for at least six weeks. During Robin's visit we agreed that Kate would go to Rozelle with the other two cats for two weeks so that she gets accustomed to being with them in different circumstances and comes to regard them as an integral part of her life. But, it now occurs to me that while this plan would probably work with Grace — who is bright and has powers of recall — it won't alter Kate's behaviour. I suspect she'll go to Rozelle with Grace and the Fluffer and will settle in quite happily once she realises the co-owners are kindly and affectionate. Then she'll return to our place and settle in equally contentedly with us. Except that by the time, four weeks later, Grace and the Fluffer return Kate will be accustomed to being sole resident cat again. I can see the wars and dramas of the winter starting all over again. It seems to me that there's only one solution.

"Kate's got to travel back and forward between the two houses with the others," I say to Michael. "They've got to be a trio. We have to co-own the lot of them."

"But Kate's our cat."

"They're all our cats," I say, emphasising the plural possessive.

"If we do that, then you won't have a cat at all when Robin and Ron are here."

"That was the original deal anyway," I point out. "Now we just won't have three cats as opposed to not having two."

"You're going off to the Academy, Kate," I tell her when she comes into our room one morning shortly afterwards. The other two aren't around. Grace has gone off to conduct serious cat business somewhere in the neighbourhood while the Fluffer's having a period of being in love with a new mat in the sitting room and prefers to have her immediate post-breakfast sleep on it, rather than in her usual position at the end of our bed. So it should have been Kate's ideal situation. She's solo cat. It's a Sunday so I have an excuse to loiter in bed. I think it's a good time to give her some undivided attention. As usual I'm feeling guilty for all the wrongs I have done her. Temporarily divorcing her. Forcing her to live with two other cats. And the really big one: letting the Fluffer supplant her place in my affections as my favourite cat. This happened without me being aware of it but now I know that when the Fluffer leaps onto the bed and comes up to say hello to me, my heart lifts. When poor Kate does the same thing, I have a tendency to look at her and say, "Oh dear, what is it this time?"

I pat my fingers on the bed to coax her up towards me for some petting. She immediately gives a wary look around as though expecting the unwanted stepsisters to materialise out of a corner and spoil her idyll. "Katie Kate," I say. "Katie cat." I try to sound soothing and affectionate and everything else a cat would wish you to be.

"You'll like the Academy," I tell her, giving her velvety ears a rub. I say, "The Academy for Smart and Decorative Cats", and reflect that something will have to be done about expanding its curriculum. An academy for smart and decorative cats doesn't really seem targeted towards Kate's needs. At the same time I don't know what I would class as Kate's defining characteristic. She's reasonably bright but she's not outstandingly intelligent like Grace and she has a pretty face and gorgeous whiskers but she's not obvious chocolate box material like the Fluffer.

What she really seems to be is a regular mainstream cat. Not entirely sane, perhaps, and with a few definite kinks (she chews paper and still has a thing about bathrooms). But if you were to advertise for a regular cat: "Prefer full-grown, affectionate moggy with pretty face and nice markings, standard cat attributes and usual range of feline idiosyncrasies", Kate would fit the bill far better than either Grace or the Fluffer.

She does regular cat business extremely well. It's Kate, for example, who catches the trio's first mouse (which turns out to be, for a long time, their only mouse — we assume that there's a lot of highly experienced local competition for the area's mice). To my relief the critical stages of this solemn event take place one evening while I'm out. I return home to be told by Michael that he noticed Kate sniffing excitedly around the bottom of the front door. Curious, he opened the door and she

Spring

immediately leapt upon the mouse. The mouse was then carried into the kitchen where she proceeded to play with it with an expertise that greatly impressed Michael. Meanwhile, the other two cats had watched enviously from a respectful distance.

"I didn't interfere," Michael says firmly. Both he and Ron are strong supporters of gun control on the one hand while believing you have to respect cats' rights as predators on the other. "And you shouldn't either," he emphasises. "In any case," he goes on, "I'm sure it's dead. I think it had a heart attack from shock. Kate's with it now under the dining table."

When I brace myself to peer under the dining table, I see Kate just sitting quietly. The real surprise is the mouse. I was expecting a standard little grey-brown creature but this is a mouse of distinction. It's dark grey and white and has black eyeliner-like markings stretching back to its ears. I'm sorry I wasn't around at the time of its capture because I would have tried to save it. I don't know if it would qualify as a "fancy mouse" but it was certainly a beautiful enough mouse to have had its own agent and considered a career on the stage. Indeed, at this point the whole mouse incident turns very theatrical because Kate apparently tires of playing with it and walks away, whereupon Grace takes over.

She's clearly been waiting all evening for this great moment. The mouse is borne out into the hall where she begins a wild game with it. As we watch in astonishment she throws it high into the air and jumps up to catch it in her mouth uttering fierce cries as she does so. Then she executes a series of vertical leaps straight upwards over its corpse. She looks as though she's auditioning for a role in some especially histrionic tribal-style ballet. It's one of the few times that I hear Michael compare her unfavourably to Kate. "For godsakes," he says to her in embarrassed-sounding tones, "you didn't catch it!"

"Here's Grace," he adds to me, "pretending she's the victorious hunter, but you should have seen Kate ..." An enthusiastic description follows of how efficient Kate had been in capturing the mouse and how skilfully she'd played with it. How she would appear to let the mouse go and then suddenly reach behind her and catch it with her paw as if she knew exactly where it would be, and so on and so forth. Meanwhile Grace exhausts herself and goes off to have a recuperative wash while the Fluffer comes over to inspect the prey. She bats it around for a bit but soon loses interest. It doesn't move and it doesn't look edible. In a quiet moment when no one, including Michael, is looking, I carry the mouse off to the garbage bin. For months afterwards I can bring Michael to a halt any time he's being disparaging about Kate by saying quellingly, "Yes, but *she* caught the mouse."

As I lie in bed and observe Kate now, I say to myself, "Ron and Robin's Academy for Smart, Decorative and Regular Cats." But then decide that, from an educational point of view, you can't have an academy for "regular" cats. You can help smart and decorative cats to become smarter and more decorative, but helping a regular cat become more "regular" sounds like a contradiction in terms. The other problem with Kate is that she's so good at learning by imitation, there never was a cat less in need of an educational institution, even an imaginary

Spring

one. She won't be the first cat to use a computer or fly an aeroplane, but she will certainly be the *second* cat to *try* to do it if the pioneering cat is so obliging as to demonstrate how it's done in front of her. "You're the world's best copycat, Katie Kate," I say to her.

Kate meanwhile has responded to being the centre of attention in an unexpected but utterly Kate-like way. Instead of sitting with me and accepting pats and purring contentedly, she's showing her delight with the situation by marching around the bed. It's as though her genetic wiring has somehow gotten crossed with that of a Lippizaner from the Spanish Riding School. She's developed a routine where I give her a pat and then she sets off ceremoniously around the edge of the bed — in a perfect rectangle, not skipping a corner — while purring enthusiastically and looking back at me over her shoulder. Then she comes up to me, gets another pat and sets off again.

After watching a dozen or so of these circuits I begin to feel slightly dizzy so I try to persuade her to come and sit with me in a more relaxed and normal fashion. She halts her march and eyes me from the end of the bed. She looks around and, after a hesitation, comes up to me. Accepts a stroke on her chin. Lowers her jaw so I'll rub her ear. Sits down next to me. Starts to purr. Plays with a bit of newspaper. Starts to chew the newspaper while I stroke her ear. Then glances towards me and as she does so, I suddenly realise what Kate's most characteristic feature is. It's an expression that says, "I know I'm going to be really unhappy in a couple of minutes."

I give her ear a rub and find myself composing a letter:

Professors Cobb and Love,
Ron and Robin's Academy
for Smart and Decorative Cats

Dear Professors,

Further to our forthcoming discussions about you admitting Kate to the Academy, I'm writing a quick note to ask if you could give consideration to expanding the curriculum to include some courses focusing on the needs of the — how can I put this? — the less optimistic type of cat.

I love Kate dearly but unfortunately she doesn't have a positive attitude to life. She expects things to go wrong and seems to make the worst of them when they do. I want to emphasise that I don't think there's anything seriously wrong with her psychologically (despite what Michael says). It's just that she's not, well, lighthearted.

If you agree to this proposal I would also like to suggest a change of name to reflect the enhanced scope of your excellent establishment. I think it ought now to be called "Ron and Robin's Academy for Smart, Decorative and Unlighthearted Cats".

Yours sincerely
Thea

Michael and I agree that the idea of including Kate in the co-ownership deal will have to be discussed with Ron and Robin, but I'm certain it's the right thing to do.

Spring

Periodically I think, what will happen if Ron and Robin stay in Sydney for a long period of time and you hardly ever see the cats? But then I reflect that I will know that they're well and happy and I'll hear news of them. What I'm really frightened of is losing a cat. I'm anxious every time the Fluffer, who's still got no road sense, gets out the front door and this anxiety, as I'm soon to discover, is about to get worse. Shortly after we return from our holiday, we learn that our landlady has decided to sell.

REAL ESTATE

Ever since somebody came up with that useful indicator of living space, room to swing a cat, there's been a link between cats and real estate. Before we start house-hunting, Michael and I have what we think is a thoroughgoing discussion about the cats' requirements and conclude that they are the same as our own. Grace, Kate and the Fluffer need a quiet street, some outdoor space — a balcony at least — and enough room indoors to move without tripping over themselves. Or, more importantly, us tripping over them.

At the beginning I think that the really important issue, as far as the cats are concerned, is traffic. Early on I see an ad for a place that sounds suitable, except that when I arrive to view it, I have an immediate flash of panic. As promised in the real estate listing, the house is "roomy; freshly painted; in a convenient location". But in those long happy years we'd spent away from the rental market,

Spring

I'd forgotten that while, in real estatese, "convenient location" does mean close to shops and public transport, it also usually means you have to cross four lanes of heavy traffic to get to them. As I stand opposite the house waiting for the lights to change, I can see the Fluffer, in the middle of one of the cats' running/chasing/jumping games, darting out that freshly painted front door just as I am going to shut it, and running straight under a car. After that I read the term "convenient location" simply as "squashed Fluffer".

I soon realise that when three of the five future tenants are feline, the situation is far more complicated than Michael and I had thought. Before long I'm refining other standard bits of real estatese to suit our circumstances. For example, I already know that the adjectives "quaint", "quirky" and "charming" mean small. However, after a couple of house inspections I become aware that quaint, quirky and charming additionally translate as "extremely cross neighbours" when all three cats go wandering from our quaint/quirky/charming courtyard into their ditto/ditto/ditto adjoining ones. "Spacious apartment with sunny balcony in small well-maintained block" soon reads to me as "Grace will go climbing in everywhere" while "designer" anything, whether kitchen, bathroom or walk-in wardrobe, is code for "no pets allowed".

In the course of all of this I discover that the most ominous description in real estatese is the one you can't decode. This enigma, which I come to term the "unexpected inclusion", is a description in a real estate listing noting some unusual feature of the property for rent. As I eventually learn, unexpected inclusions are usually completely accurate about whatever it is they are describing. But what they actually mean is that there's something else, quite unrelated, which is terribly wrong with the property.

My favourite example of the genre is the phrase "level walk to station" in a listing for a pleasant-sounding, well-located, single-storey house with "spacious front and rear gardens". I decide that maybe, in this era of the expanding forty-plus demographic, the agent's trying to pitch the property at an older commuter couple. As I set off to view the place, I spend half my time happily imagining this contented commuter couple (they're rather like Michael and me, except they've got regular incomes) and the other half thinking how much Grace, Kate and the Fluffer would enjoy playing in those spacious front and rear gardens. Then I arrive at the house and discover that "level walk to station" actually means "overlooked on all sides by multi-storey apartment blocks".

As narratives, my experiences of house-hunting have been remarkably similar. There's always been the ideal-place-I-miss-out-on just when I begin the search. This time it's a surprisingly cheap, pleasant, well-presented house and for weeks afterwards it's a constant sad presence in my mind. I make unfavourable comparisons between it and every other place I see and have fantasies about the tenants who got it having to relocate suddenly to Noumea. As usual this phase is followed by a very grim period when I see a range of houses all of which are dank, dirty and badly renovated thirty years ago.

One day, in the middle of the very grim period, it occurs to me as I'm going from one unfortunate place to another

Spring

that I am no longer looking at houses for rent. What's happened is that I've had a parallel universe type experience and am now living inside a gritty inner-city police drama. The last three houses I've seen are squats for drug addicts while the one with the best parking will also be where the undercover cop has his or her inevitable moral crisis. The three bedroom townhouse I saw earlier in the day, which had bars everywhere, is the safe house for the informer under police protection. However, the informer will have to get executed in the combined dining/sitting room as there's no likelihood of simultaneously fitting the victim, the shooter and the gun into any other room in the house.

After a day spent cruising my police drama locations, I come home one evening and announce to the cats, "Saw a great place for a serial killer this afternoon. No natural light but a huge backyard not overlooked by any neighbours where you could bury dismembered bodies to your heart's content."

The cats turn towards me with sated, dreamy gazes. They have just had their dinner, conducted the late evening round of battles and are now contemplating their next wash. Despite the fact that they were all abandoned kittens who — but for human intervention — would have been living their own versions of a gritty inner-city life, none of them look like they would be at home anywhere except in the sort of nice Paddington terrace which is now rapidly moving out of their co-owners' price range. I go to bed feeling very depressed.

Fortunately The House appears soon afterwards. It's close to the city, in a Surry Hills cul-de-sac. The woodwork needs a coat of paint and the carpets look like they've been through a civil war, but it has pleasant rooms, a roof garden and a big tree at the front. The minute I see it, I imagine the cats and us having serene evenings on the roof admiring the city lights. I see Grace contently climbing to the very tip of the big tree. I see us all being happy together in the sunny bedroom on winter mornings. I become so desperate to get The House that, as far as the letting agency's concerned, I propose entirely suppressing the existences of Kate, Grace and the Fluffer. Michael, though, disagrees. "A lot of people have cats," he points out. "It could be more awkward if they found out later we hadn't been telling the truth."

"Does the landlord object to cats?" I ask with feigned casualness at the agency when we go to lodge our application.

"How many cats do you have?"

"Two."

We have two cats according to a formula I've developed where if you have three cats on a part time basis, this would work out as two cats full time. It's the feline equivalent of what is called by labour market statisticians Effective Full-time Positions. I have a feeling that most landlords would regard two cats as company, but would consider three cats as too many cats.

"I'm sure it'll be alright," says the real estate agent, who's very pleasant, "as long as they're clean."

I realise I have to reassure her on this point even though it's clear she's got enough experience and agent-savvy to know that in all the collected annals of real estate, there has never been such a thing as a tenant knowingly

Spring

afflicted with a dirty cat. When anyone talks, though, about a cat being "clean" I immediately imagine this superior animal who stalks into its owner's presence one morning and announces, "I believe this business of taking my wet tongue out of my mouth and running it over my fur and putting it back into my mouth again is unhygienic and ought to stop. I would like you to put in place appropriate alternative arrangements for my personal laundering."

At the same time I'm hesitant because, strictly speaking, our cats are not clean. Well, they do their toilets where they're supposed to, though they make it obvious they'd much prefer a freshly dug garden bed or a pot plant newly filled with quality potting mix. Moreover, they are all what can only be described as serial washers, even if there are occasions when we feel that the assiduous licking that's currently underway has little to do with personal hygiene and a great deal to do with the lamp that is lying on its side in the sitting room.

The problem is that they all seem to get into various sorts of dirt. The Fluffer's tail is a magnet for cobwebs and if these don't get extracted through her normal washing processes, she adopts an aristocratic hauteur when you approach her with the cat brush to help out: "Cobwebs? Cobwebs! I don't see any cobwebs. Take that thing away, I like to be stroked by hand."

Grace's difficulty is her fondness for alpine walks. Inevitably her voyages involve trips across the tops of high cupboards that usually only get cleaned when we're expecting visitors ten feet tall and over, so her paws acquire a layer of thoroughly integrated dust and grime which promptly gets transferred to the next surface on which she walks.

Kate, meanwhile, is on a personal mission to explore as many Victorian fireplaces as possible and if the access to the chimney isn't properly sealed, she thrusts her way in and re-emerges spotted with coal dust, powdered bird droppings, semi-decayed insect parts and various other things I'd rather not describe but which can, somehow, get into the lower levels of a disused chimney.

"Still," I tell myself, "the cats themselves aren't dirty. They are just prone to occasions of dirt. If there were no fireplaces, no high ledges and no obscure corners in which cobwebs can congregate, they would be fine."

I'm aware that none of this applies to The House, which has even more old fireplaces, alpine cupboards and tiny corners to besmirch the Fluffer's tail than our present house, but we all, cats and humans alike, need a home.

I say firmly, "They are very clean cats."

THEME PARKS
FOR CATS

The next week is spent packing up the Paddington house. The cats are enthralled by the upheaval. They climb into empty boxes, sit on top of packs of files and regard the whole business as being staged solely for their amusement. This comes as no surprise to me because I had already been through a couple of experiences of spring-cleaning with their assistance.

The first spring-cleaning episode was the cupboard under the stairs. This had become a repository for things which we no longer used but couldn't resolve to get rid of, and things which were in the way and had been put under the stairs until a more suitable home could be found. What was wonderful was that over the years these categories had merged. Everything has become expendable.

So when I finally stop postponing the clean-up, I discover I have quite an easy job. Just sort into give-away and total-rubbish. Clean and pack the give-aways neatly. Bag the rubbish. Sweep, dust and mop the cupboard. Install new contents of cupboard in a rational manner. A few hours work at the outside. Until the cats arrive.

Grace, Kate and the Fluffer have always known about this cupboard. It's near their feeding dishes and on occasion a cat has managed to insert herself into it. "Insert" is the appropriate word. The cupboard is so jam-packed that even the cats have to burrow their way through it to get around. Kate, inevitably, got herself locked in once and set off a missing cat crisis until we heard a pathetic meow.

But they've never before had a full-scale chance to explore it and now they can't believe their good fortune. With wide eyes they watch me as I pile objects out of the cupboard for them to examine. I soon discover that wherever I attempt to put a foot there is already a cat undertaking an inspection. The Fluffer crawls into every container. I glance around and see that an old skirt on top of a box of clothes is starting to heave and realise that I've dropped it in on top of her. Kate discovers an inordinate number of objects which she can bat gently around the floor. Grace climbs onto each pile of goods and watches my every movement with an expression on her thin intelligent face that says I will never cease to amaze her.

But the fun of all this is immediately forgotten when they realise that by emptying the cupboard, I'm creating a new space. A perfect cat-sized space which they have never been aware existed. Each one goes into the cupboard,

Spring

comes out and then looks at me as if to say, "I didn't know *this* was here." I can see their point. They think they're familiar with every inch of the house: they have gotten onto shelves, crawled into wardrobes, emerged from under beds with an embarrassing amount of fluff in their whiskers and yet here is this whole new territory. Thrilled and incredulous, they go in again and again for another survey of this just-discovered wonder. "It's as if," I report crossly to Michael later in the day, "I'd just set up their own private theme park. They were so excited that none of them went off for their midday sleep. They just spent the entire time crawling into and over everything and getting in my way."

Indeed, the only good thing I could say of my first experience of spring-cleaning with the cats was that it did inspire me to develop a new theory of feline domestication. The standard explanations for how this happened connect it with the expansion of agriculture in Egypt. The Egyptians started storing their harvests in granaries, which naturally attracted rats and the rats attracted cats, so soon you had thriving cat colonies around the granaries. This situation continued for an undetermined period of time until one day a cat with Grace's intelligence and huge appetite was pondering the formula of Egyptians + granaries + rats = food 4 cats and realised that if you deleted those messy bits in the middle, you would come up with the elegantly simple equation of Egyptians = food 4 cats. My revised theory is that domestication happened immediately after the invention of furniture. "Wow," said the cats of prehistory, gathering around bright-eyed and impressed at their first sight of a chest of drawers, "that looks like fun. Let's move in with people."

House-moving day is the usual high-speed mixture of giving directions and answering questions while rapidly and mindlessly wrapping items in paper, stuffing them in boxes, sealing the boxes and starting the process all over again. Through it all I worry about the cats. Before the movers arrive, we lock them in the laundry from which everything has already been cleared. They will hear the noise of the movers, but they're accustomed to being shut up in the laundry when we have tradesmen in the house and usually simply sleep through the upheaval. Once we're settled in the Surry Hills house with the furniture in place and the removalists gone, Michael will return to Paddington to fetch them.

I've put together my own recipe for rehousing cats by combining the advice from various cat books. "When they arrive," I explain to Michael, "we must focus on soothing them. We have to be calm. We should stop organising and unpacking and sit down and talk to them." He agrees. He has already vetoed another cat adviser's suggestion that we don't feed the cats prior to moving so they will be more eager to eat and — the idea is — to settle in their new home by saying, "It sounds like torture. They're going to have a bad enough day as it is without being hungry too."

Like everything else that happens on the moving day, my cat plans work about a tenth as well in practice as in theory. Due to a timing miscalculation on my part, the kitchen in the new house still has a mound of wrapping

Spring

paper on the floor when Michael arrives bearing the pet carriers. When they emerge, though, none of the cats seems to even notice the small mountain of butcher's paper. Instead they stand, backs arched, heads forward, peering about them, utterly astonished.

It's clear some things compute. Michael and I are here. Their familiar food dishes are on the floor before them. They must recognise the smells of our kitchenware, crockery and furniture. But everything else is strange. For a few minutes the three stand in the middle of the room, all staring in different directions, their muscles rigid and their eyes bulging to the edges of their sockets. They look as if they've just crash-landed on a different planet.

Faced with this collective astonishment it takes me a minute to remember I'm supposed to be in reassurance mode. I should be calm and soothing. "Good pussycats," I say. I don't feel at all calm and am certain I don't sound soothing but I dispense pats and praise and push their food dishes towards them. Kate and the Fluffer, whose joint idea of paradise it usually is to be stroked and petted while they eat, completely ignore both the food and me.

Grace meanwhile looks at us in outrage, as if to say, "I knew you two were up to something. But I never imagined it was anything like *this*!"

After that she stalks off to explore the rest of the house and I suddenly realise we've completely forgotten the other bit of our cat rehousing strategy. "We're supposed to familiarise them gradually with their new environment," I say despairingly to Michael. "We should have kept them in one closed room and then let them go into other rooms in stages as they got used to the house."

"Well, we couldn't have done that anyway," he answers, "because we've got the electrician crawling all over the place."

I give up on cat-soothing. They are clearly cats who don't see soothing as appropriate. They aren't interested in calm. Their whole world has been upended and they just want to deal with it in their own way. My attempts at comfort are irrelevant. I gather together the mountain of wrapping paper, finish the essential unpacking in the kitchen and go upstairs to make way for the electrician, who is checking the wiring of the kitchen ceiling lights.

Upstairs my first priority is to find the blankets. The day has become chilly and the sky is darkening for a storm. I'm nearly finished making the bed and am just laying the cover over it when Grace walks in. She leaps up onto the bed, arranges herself in her usual position in the corner and, after a glance at me, starts to wash. My heart lifts in relief. Our bed has always been her refuge. When the weather turns cold suddenly or the house fills up with visitors, she has always gone into our bedroom to sleep. She is now starting to look frankly impatient. She wants me to be finished with the bed so that she can settle down to a thorough wash and a nap. A minute or two later her face assumes that half-alert, half-mesmerised look she gets when she's washing. "Well, you're alright," I say happily, "aren't you?"

Then the door opens and the Fluffer appears. She jumps up onto the bed near Grace. I give them both a pat and tell them they are wonderful, perfect, clever cats. The Fluffer starts to purr. Outside the rain begins.

I am always more aware of the weather in new houses.

Spring

In this house the change is more dramatic than usual because I can hear the rain landing heavily on the skylights. As recommended in the cat communication manuals, I lie down so that my face is on a level with those of Grace and the Fluffer and I tell them again and again what wonderful, perfect etc. cats they are. For a few minutes we engage in an exchange of purrings, rubbings, admirings and assorted gestures of affection until I hear Michael downstairs calling their names.

"They are up here," I say, getting up to go and lean over the stairs where I can talk to him. "And looking very contented with their new circumstances."

"Where's Kate?"

I realise I've been expecting Kate to appear in the bedroom in the wake of the other two. I say I haven't seen her for the last half hour or so and come down the stairs calling to her. Michael begins interrogating the electrician, who assures us that no, he hasn't left the front door open and no, he definitely hasn't let a cat out the front door. "She will be hiding in a box," he says to us while climbing a ladder to examine the light fitting in the hall. "I've just come from another house where the same thing happened. The cat went missing when the family moved in. They found her in a box."

I'm doubtful. I say that Kate is a clinger rather than a hider, the Fluffer is the one who crawls into things when she's frightened, while Kate tends to follow us around, wailing. But I go around nonetheless peering into boxes and calling her name. There are at least twenty boxes scattered through the house in various stages of being semi-opened, half-full and near-empty. Kate isn't in any of them.

The Cat Who Looked at the Sky

"The door onto the roof is shut, isn't it?" I ask Michael.

"I closed it when it started to rain."

"You mean it hasn't been locked all the time? I thought you said a while ago that it was!"

We are both thinking the same thing. Kate could have gotten out onto the roof, climbed down to a neighbour's roof and run away. From his ladder in the background, the electrician intones his advice: she'll be hiding in a box.

We hurry up the stairs, pausing for a second to check on the other cats and make sure that Kate hasn't joined them. The two of them are now settled down, personal laundries completed, and looking very serene.

On the roof the rain is hurtling down, heavy drops ricocheting off the slat wood flooring. Above we can see large clouds still massing. It is obviously going to rain for hours. We can't remember where any of our coats or umbrellas are, so we just go out into the rain and walk around the roof wall calling Kate's name. I'm confident that any minute she's going to appear but all that happens is that the rain gets heavier.

We go back into the house and I search all the boxes and cupboards again, calling as I do so. Then I return to the roof and stand in the doorway and call to Kate, thinking that if she has climbed onto a neighbouring roof and is frightened of making her way back, hearing my voice will encourage her. I'm still expecting her to come crawling over the roof wall at any minute, with her fur all wet and flattened from the rain, and looking aggrieved in her usual fashion that suggests I'm somehow always responsible for anything bad that happens to her. But after

Spring

a quarter of an hour I have to give up and return downstairs. I can't believe that she's run away, but then she is, as Michael says, emotional, unpredictable, prone to overreacting.

"She's gone back to the old house," he now announces with finality.

"I was more worried about the other two than her," I say, starting, as usual, to feel guilty. "I thought somehow that they'd be the ones who'd be really upset."

It now appears obvious to me that Kate should have been my primary concern. Grace and the Fluffer are more accustomed to being moved. "Besides," I add, thinking of the two of them together on the bed upstairs, "they have each other."

I console myself with the thought that we expect to be going back to the Paddington house constantly during the next week and we can alert the neighbours. If Kate returns, we can fetch her back.

"When I was young," Michael says to me and the electrician who seems to have become a participant in our crisis, "we had a cat who ran back to our old house three times. We finally had to give up and get the new people to adopt her."

Both the electrician and I respond to this story with noncommittal nods. I can believe that Kate would run away once in panic, but I can't see her persisting in doing so. The electrician meanwhile is still convinced she's safe somewhere in the house. In a box.

As I go on unpacking I can't stop thinking about poor Kate. I imagine her making her way back to Paddington in the rain. The city is wet and cold and grey. A block away there's a major road with peak hour traffic sweeping down the hill towards the Harbour Bridge. Another block and there's another major road jammed this time of day with buses. Nobody will notice a little, wet grey-brown cat running desperately across a busy road on such a stormy evening. A quick swipe by a speeding car and she'll be in a gutter with her back broken.

Yet this prospect doesn't distress me as much as the thought of how she must be feeling. The cat advice books I've read had various theories about why and how cats find their way back to former homes, but none of them talked about the cat's state of mind while she is making her journey. However impelled she's feeling, whatever ingrained maps in her memory she is following, I can't believe that my affection-hungry, demanding, dependent Kate is in some way so anaesthetised by her instincts that she is oblivious to her surroundings. I keep thinking of her running along the strange, rainy, terrifying streets in an agony of panic.

Every real estate agent, tradesman or removalist we've encountered during the previous few days seems to spend half their time answering their mobile phones, and the electrician's no exception. But he keeps on working while he talks. As I'm arranging the bookshelves in the sitting room I can hear him discussing a problem with a client. He's standing on top of his ladder with the phone tucked into his neck while using both hands to unscrew, check and replace lights fittings. He asks questions in a gentle, quiet way, gives some advice about how to handle the problem in the short term, repeats all his directions carefully and patiently, and only says, right at the end of

Spring

the conversation, that he is actually six feet up a ladder at the moment and can't check his appointments but will ring the caller back as soon as he can.

After he conducts a couple more conversations along similar lines, I begin to imagine a scene in which some kindly person finds Kate, discovers her owners through the microchip register and rings us to ask if we've lost a cat. I'm in the middle of a conversation with this kindly person and have just reached the point of asking (for it's the most definite way, sight unseen, of identifying Kate), "When she jumps off things, does she make a sort of hee-umph noise?" when I realise what, or more correctly who, has inspired all this.

The electrician is one of life's natural calmers and soothers. I had started feeling better just from overhearing him talk and begun making up a happy fantasy about finding Kate as a result. (Later on I'm a bit puzzled as to why I had a question about identifying Kate when her identity had already been established through the microchip, but I guess I was just getting carried away with the narrative.) I bring the fantasy to a halt, but my mood improves. I start feeling optimistic. I remind myself that while Kate is intense and emotional, she can look after herself. She's never climbed up to places from which she can't get down, nor has she run out in front of cars. Later on I tell Michael that we should have hired our kindly electrician not to redo the wiring but to settle the cats in. "And us too, for that matter."

That evening around seven, I'm walking down the narrow back hall towards the kitchen when I see a movement in the shadowy space below the stairs and a familiar brown and grey figure emerges. "Hel-lo, Kate," I say. "Glad you could join us."

"Rainy storm-swept streets of the city indeed!" I add to myself sarcastically.

The electrician was almost right. She wasn't actually hiding in a box but behind the empty boxes. All through the long hours while I'd been fretting about her running in terror back to Paddington, I had been flattening boxes as I emptied them, and pushing them into the opening of the storage space under the stairs, unaware that she was curled up, presumably asleep, on a shelf behind them.

The following afternoon I'm more prepared. When the TV installer uses a drill and all the cats disappear, I know immediately where to look for Kate. I put my head over the row of boxes and call her name. Two small voices answer me, and in the darkness I can see two sets of eyes. Kate has taken the Fluffer with her into her hidey-hole and the two of them are curled up together on a back shelf having a joint kitten regression.

COCKTAIL HOUR

In our first days in the new house the event we most dread is to have any of the cats, but most particularly the Fluffer, go missing. While our new street is a cul-de-sac, it's near to the city so drivers jostle in it all day for short term parking and there is often traffic in the lane at the side of the house. As a result I'm constantly checking the cats' whereabouts, even when it's obvious they are doing nothing more dangerous than making their way languidly from their food dishes to the sitting room sofa. Accordingly, it's a major drama when we wake one morning about a week after moving in and find that Grace and the Fluffer have gotten out of the house through a broken window screen.

It's still early when we discover the pair are missing and I keep telling myself two things: (a) that Grace will come back for her breakfast, and (b) she will bring the Fluffer home with her. I put out their meals with the maximum amount of attendant noise: fridge-openings, spoons

The Cat Who Looked at the Sky

clattering against cans, dry food rattling in plastic dishes plus conversation with Kate, who hasn't followed the others out of the window and is, I suspect, rather enjoying being solo cat at meal time. Shortly afterwards, in confirmation of my theory, Grace appears.

Michael, who has been watching the front of the house, doesn't see her enter so we assume she's come down the stairs after climbing up from the side lane to the roof. We hope that the Fluffer has followed and immediately go up to check but there's no sign of the little black cat. We walk around the sides of the roof calling to her and then go back downstairs and call to her from each of the windows and the front balcony. When there's no answering meow, Michael goes to dress so he can start searching the nearby streets and asking the neighbours. I stand on the front balcony. The streets are quiet. Peak hour is still some time away, but I keep remembering what Robin said months before: "It only takes one." It's an unfamiliar neighbourhood, the Fluffer could panic and run out in front of a car in the side lane, a driver wouldn't notice her in the dim early morning light.

I'm just up to this point in my grim scenario when I remind myself that (a) we have a clear view of the side lane and (b) if the Fluffer has been hit by a car, we would have found her, or seen hair or blood. I tell myself firmly that Grace got back into the house by climbing up onto the roof and that the Fluffer will follow Grace — it will take her longer but she will follow — so I go back up to the roof again and start calling. Kate hangs around my legs, meowing loudly every time I call the Fluffer's name.

Suddenly there's a loud thump behind me and I turn to

Spring

see that the Fluffer has landed on the slat flooring of the roof. Her fur is full of cobwebs and small blue buds from the plumbago hedge in the side lane. The trip up to the roof by whatever necessary combination of climbs and jumps across neighbours' balconies and roofs has clearly frightened her, and we suspect, from the amount of time we have to spend removing bits of plumbago from her lavish tail, that at one point she must have fallen into the hedge. Unlike Grace, who eats her breakfast with her usual enthusiasm, the Fluffer isn't interested in food. In fact it takes her all day to recover her composure and become her usual sweetly serene and absent-minded self again, but this doesn't worry us. We are so relieved that she's home, and furthermore that she knows how to climb up the wall into the house even if the journey terrifies her.

After this experience I resolve that I'll stop fearing the worst every time something untoward happens with the cats in their new home. But when Kate disappears again a few days later, it takes quite some time before I remember that I'm supposed to stay calm and assume our cats are capable of looking after themselves.

This drama happens the day that the carpet layers come to replace the carpet on the stairs. We had planned to shut the cats up in the dining and sitting rooms. These two large rooms open into each other and have quickly become the cats' favourite part of the house. They take their daily siestas there, Grace in the carver chair at the head of the dining table, Kate in a lounge chair in front of the TV and the Fluffer curled up somewhere on the floor. When you walk in at midday each of the cats is so still and so soundly asleep it's as though the room is under a spell.

The Cat Who Looked at the Sky

It emerges at the last minute, though, that the carpet layers need these rooms for their equipment, so the trio have to be locked out on the roof area. This makes me anxious because they aren't yet accustomed to going on the roof. When we decided to rent the house we had thought of the roof garden as being one of its prime attractions. We imagined the cats happily climbing the lattice-covered walls, setting off to explore neighbouring roofs, surveying the street below from their private eyrie and dozing contentedly in the small sunroom. But, during the first weeks we are in the new house the weather is cold and wet. Kate and the Fluffer give the roof a cursory inspection and after that ignore it while Grace, who's usually adventurous, avoids it.

I know why she does. Just after our arrival she followed me up onto the roof. One of the magpies which nest in the tall trees in the street had swooped down towards us. Grace quailed and I suddenly had a cat's eye view of the world. She was in a strange, exposed place and the sky above was full of creatures bigger than she was who could descend upon her without warning. If I had been her I would have been frightened too.

The morning of the carpet laying she begins to struggle when she realises where I'm taking her. As usual, I immediately feel guilty. "I'm sorry," I say to her as she writhes in my arms, "if we'd known what was going to happen, we would have taken you up here earlier and soothed and settled you in with food and petting." Adding the standard rationalisation, "It's not for very long," I push her outside and lock the glass door. She makes a desperate run for the door as it closes. Imprisoning the other two cats is less dramatic but afterwards all three of them stare

Spring

angrily at me through the glass. I give them standard rationalisation number two: "It's for your own good." As I'm leaving I tell myself that they have food and water. There are plenty of places for them to sleep. The weather is finally starting to clear, it looks as though it's going to be a sunny day. They might even go exploring.

It is only afterwards that I realise how terrifying the carpet laying must have been for the cats. First there would have been a period of mayhem when they could see through the glass door that strange men had arrived and were ripping up the coverings of the stairs. But this racket wouldn't have lasted for very long. It would have been followed by a period of relative quiet while the carpet layers checked measurements and organised materials, but then something truly frightening would have taken place. The carpet layers started in the hall and worked upwards to the roof. This meant that the cats would have heard coming towards them a loud and alien sound made up of the combined noises of hammers, staple guns, flattening machines, strange human voices and constantly ringing mobile phones. At the beginning it would have been frightening enough, but at least distant. Then it would have drawn inexorably closer to finally culminate in an earsplitting half hour while the carpet was being relaid on the landing just inside the roof door.

I become aware of how serious things were when I go up to the roof after the carpet layers have gone and instead of being welcomed as I expect by a trio of cross but relieved cats, I can't see any of them.

"Well, they must all be together," Michael remarks when I report this to him. He comes upstairs with me and we walk around the roof carrying out the now familiar routine of scanning the neighbours' roofs and calling again and again to the cats After ten minutes or so there is an answering cry and after a further baffling ten minutes, during which we keep hearing cries from some point over our heads, Michael finds Grace. Her neat triangle of a face is poking out of a gap below the eaves of the sunroom. Terrified by the noise of the carpet laying, she found a small space to hide between the ceiling and the roof of the sunroom and crawled in and, as we eventually discover, took the Fluffer with her. After half an hour Michael manages to coax the pair of them out.

The next problem is the whereabouts of Kate. We know from observing her reactions to the noise of large trucks in the street that she isn't as sensitive to sounds as the other two. So initially I'm quite confident she'll reappear soon. Indeed, through all the time we spend persuading the other two out of their hiding place I keep expecting her to emerge from some corner. But even after Grace and the Fluffer have been rescued, petted and fed, there's no sign of her. Michael has to go back to work so I continue the search.

I know that there are only two places where she can be. Either, like the other two cats, she's concealed herself somewhere on our roof or she's on a neighbour's roof. It doesn't seem to me that there are many places where a cat could hide on our roof but after discovering Grace and the Fluffer in a space which Michael and I didn't realise existed, I'm aware that my concept of topography is totally different from a cat's. I call out, examine every nook and cranny and eventually conclude that she's somewhere on a neighbour's roof.

Spring

Our house is at the top of a rise overlooking a short row of terrace houses but my view of the neighbours' roofs is obscured by chimneys, attic windows and satellite dishes. It's a hot late afternoon. People haven't begun returning from work yet and, apart from the hum of traffic in the distance, everything is quiet and still. I'm sure that Kate can hear me calling and I find myself feeling both anxious and exasperated. I keep remembering how I was convinced she'd run away the day we moved and then she'd emerged, calm as you please, for her dinner. I tell myself firmly that she will do exactly the same this time. But then I keep thinking, what if she doesn't … ? Some of the neighbouring roofs are steep and dangerous. She would have been agitated by the strange voices and noises. Cats can fall.

Soon I'm thinking, it's just like when we moved, I was more worried then about Grace and the Fluffer than I was about her. I always assume, on no real evidence, that she can handle crises better than they can. I feel simultaneously guilty about underestimating the impact of the situation on her, irritated at her for not responding to my call, and frightened that she might have slipped on some weather-damaged roof tiles on a neighbouring house and is now lying somewhere with broken bones, able to hear me calling but unable to cry loudly enough for me to hear her.

In the course of all this it occurs to me how often I feel this mixture of anxiety, exasperation and guilt about Kate as compared to the other two cats, and I suddenly see she is the character in the narrative who makes things come undone. If there was just Grace and the Fluffer, I'd spend my time admiring Grace and adoring the Fluffer. Nice but static, no conflict. Once Kate arrives, though, you've got a story. The best laid plans go awry because she's emotional, excessive, won't follow orders, is the designated wild card. Faced with what she perceived as danger it would have made perfect sense to Grace not to take Kate into the hiding place with her and the Fluffer. Grace knows she can manage the Fluffer, but she can't manage Kate. In a crisis Kate could get them all shot.

As I peer out at the neighbours' roofs I'm mentally casting Kate in half a dozen movies. She's the gang member who ruins the perfect heist by gunning down the guard; she's the kidnapper who, at the last moment, refuses to shoot the victim (and naturally gets killed herself by the police); she's the — well, you can see the pattern. All this diverts me enough to stop my panic. I begin to think about the house-moving day and realise what we should do. The sun is starting to set. The time has come to move into calm-and-soothing mode.

I go downstairs to Michael's office and outline my strategy: "I'm sure Kate's around somewhere but she's too frightened to leave her hidey-hole and I suspect my calling to her is simply making her more agitated. I think that what we ought to do is go up on the roof and have a glass of wine and a chat. She must be getting hungry and if she hears us talking away as though everything is normal, she will come out."

In retrospect this proposal looks more like an excuse for Michael and me to open a bottle of wine than the first thing a pair of concerned owners should do when faced with a missing and presumably traumatised cat. But, we'd been packing and cleaning and unpacking and cleaning day in and day out for the past two weeks and we were running out of energy for cat crises.

It's also the first afternoon since we'd moved in that it's been fine enough for us to sit outdoors. "Cocktail hour on the roof," Michael announces to Grace and the Fluffer, who are hanging around his feet as he puts a bottle of wine and glasses on a tray. They have already had their evening meal but as usual they're convinced that any new human activity in the kitchen will somehow be linked to the provision of extra food for them, so they follow us up to the roof where we sit and sip our wine and feel like we're in a low-budget version of a scene familiar from a million advertisements. Relaxed couple enjoying pre-dinner drinks on terrace with city vista in background. The sort of owners any fraught but fixated cat would want to come home to.

Grace and the Fluffer watch us for a time and then start exploring in a desultory way. Grace gets onto the sunroom roof with a series of easy leaps and peers down at us. The Fluffer carefully climbs a lattice wall and looks immensely proud of herself. She then climbs carefully down again and looks immensely relieved to be back on the ground. As Michael and I watch the lights of distant aeroplanes in the darkening evening sky, the Fluffer discovers that if she jumps onto a chair, she can then jump onto the table and from there she can easily climb onto the chest-high wall at the edge of the roof.

Grace, of course, can leap onto the wall in a single bound but the Fluffer has never quite got a grip on this

The Cat Who Looked at the Sky

business of jumping-up-and-down and climbing-up-and-over. She much prefers the horizontal and was delighted at Paddington when our next door neighbours, in the course of excavations to build a garage, removed their fences and installed a gangplank at ground level, which permitted her to leave our backyard, stroll effortlessly across theirs and then, equally effortlessly, get onto the balcony at the rear of the next house. You could see her thinking, well, this sure beats having to scramble up and down all those fences.

Now that she's on the wall, though, she faces a jump down to the neighbour's roof. As she sits and contemplates this, I hear a thump behind me accompanied by a familiar 'hee-umph' noise. Kate's landing sound. I turn around, say hello and give her a pat. We don't see where she has come from but she had obviously found herself a refuge on a neighbour's roof. We open another bottle of wine to celebrate her return and the success of our strategy while she heads off to her dinner bowl.

The upshot of this evening is unexpected. The following evening around the same time I'm lying on the bed half reading the paper and half reviewing all the tasks still to be done when I become aware that the Fluffer is acting oddly. She's on the landing outside the door to the bedroom, hanging around the way that cats do when they want you to do something: feed them; sit down so that they can have a curl-up on your lap; get off their favourite chair so they can have a sleep. First I think she is hungry, but then I remember that I heard the sequence of noises that signifies the cats'

Spring

dinner: cupboards opening, rattle of dry food hitting plastic bowls, rapid patter of Grace's feet as she scurries across the polished floorboards of Michael's office on her way to eat.

I study the Fluffer as she wanders around the freshly carpeted landing. Clearly a cat with something on her mind. For once, looking at her gives me no pleasure. This isn't her fault. The old carpet on the stairs was the same aged dusty rose pink as the carpet in the sitting and dining rooms downstairs. The carpet that has replaced it is of a shade of pink best described as "bordello vehement". The sight of it immediately puts me in mind of curvy women in lacy underwear and six-inch heels. The problem is that it's the first floor covering I have seen that the Fluffer doesn't enhance. The contrast between her black fur and the vehement pink makes the carpet look even more lurid while the poor Fluffer herself looks like an accessory in a softcore porn shot.

When Michael comes in a few minutes later, I point to her and say, "They've all been fed, haven't they?"

He nods. He looks at the Fluffer. "She wants us to go up on the roof."

I raise my eyebrows at this latest example of cat tyranny but we go up onto the roof to watch the sunset and I soon see that he's right. The Fluffer has developed a sense of adventure — at the luxury end of the market. She would go on safari, for example, but expect to take her own chef and personal stylist. Grace and Kate come up to join us once they become aware of what's happening but it's the Fluffer who has been the first to realise that a cat can have a very pleasant time on the roof in the cool of the evening, so long as the humans are there to scare away any threatening birds. As we watch her tentatively setting off to explore the surrounding rooftops, Michael observes, "The Fluffer's a thoroughgoing hedonist."

SUMMER/
AUTUMN

THUG PRINCESS

All the cats are now over a year old and we think that they are fully and officially mature. But then, as we report to their co-owners in Los Angeles, we notice that both Grace and Kate have been growing. Kate seems to be only a little bit bigger. But Grace's frame has grown altogether larger and her legs have become longer and stronger. She's now in proportion again and while we know her midriff could be more concave, we no longer worry about putting her on a diet. At the same time her coat, which was mostly brown when she was a kitten, has gradually grown darker and is now largely black with bright flashes of ginger and tan. Our new neighbours call her "the Burmese cat" and say she's beautiful. However, the most dramatic changes have taken place with the Fluffer.

The first sign, though we don't realise it at the time, is that the Fluffer starts to talk. This happens during the period while we're settling into the new house. Having a cat who's only ever meowed half a dozen times suddenly begin vocalising is so unexpected that at first I don't even register it's happening. One morning the Fluffer comes running into our bedroom and utters a couple of cries. I'm busy, trying to get the basic housekeeping chores out of the way so I can finish unpacking. I say, "Hello, Fluffer, hello, darling," and bend down to give her a pat. She twines around my leg while I stroke her neck, then leaps onto the bed I'm making to get some more petting until I distract her by putting her on the windowsill where she can watch the side lane. It's only afterwards I remember that when she came into the room, the Fluffer was making what was recognisably a greeting cry.

Over the next few weeks it becomes apparent that she has the full range of significant meows. She can do a suitably indignant, "Where's my dinner?" and "Let me in!" as well as a forlorn and desolate, *"Where is everybody?"* when she wakes up and no one seems to be around. All this makes me gaze at her wondering if she could always talk but just didn't feel the urge or if this is some final stage of her development. I keep mentally trailing back through the pile of cat-raising manuals that used to live by my bedside trying to remember if there was ever any information about cats who didn't meow.

I finally decide that it is developmental one day when I see her on the roof giving a series of little cries as she watches a bird. Her cry is not as distinctive as the chuk-chuk noise Grace makes when she's preparing to stalk, but it obviously serves the same function. But that doesn't entirely settle the matter because by then I've discovered that as well as meowing, the Fluffer has started having conversations. When she comes into my office she meows in a chatty sort of way and I reply. Then she meows a few more times and I make a couple more comments as seems appropriate. Pretty much a standard conversation to have with a cat, except that it's a complete mystery to me what we are talking about.

It isn't so difficult understanding Grace and Kate. Grace makes her cheep-cheep noise when she's agitated — from being accidentally locked out, for example — otherwise she relies entirely on body language. I get the impression she could talk if she wanted to but suggesting she communicate by meows would be a bit like telling some great ballerina that an audience would enjoy her performance more if she would just utter a few lines of dialogue now and again.

Kate's conversations invariably sound like complaints. Michael manages talks with her by saying sympathetically at intervals, "I know, I know." I say, "Oh dear, Kate, isn't that terrible?", and give her a pat on the head (forgetting that she dislikes being patted on the head) and tell her that I hope things will get better soon. After which she gazes up at me with big hurt eyes and I (predictably) feel guilty.

When the Fluffer talks, though, it doesn't sound like either a demand or a complaint. Instead it often sounds as if she's resuming a conversation we started earlier. The first noise she makes will usually be brief, as though she is saying, "Hello!/There you are!/Isn't it hot?" But the second cry will be longer and more complex and sound rather like a sentence. Except what the Fluffer could be composing sentences about is quite beyond me. Is she observing that from time to time she feels overcome by a primordial urge to pursue, torture and consume small birds and rodents? I suppose so, but think it sounds a bit abstract for the Fluffer.

Is she reporting that she has won all her wrestles with Kate this morning and managed to bite her quite fiercely a couple of times in the process? Possibly. But as she usually wins all her fights with the other cats, and can actually take on Grace and Kate simultaneously and still win, it would surprise me that she'd bother to mention it. Also, at this time in the complicated world of cat politics, the Fluffer seems so unassuming and so accepting of her apparent position at the bottom of the pecking order that we are not even sure she's aware there is a big discrepancy between her lowly position and the fact that she can beat both the other cats up.

Is she saying something appreciative about the salmon cutlets that we had for dinner last night? This sounds more likely. As usual, the previous evening the Fluffer sat and watched us eat our dinner while the other two cats went off about their own activities, and, as usual, she ended the night by having a gourmet supper all to herself of grilled salmon skin. The more I think about it, the more I figure that, yes, it's food that the Fluffer's talking about. She'd know there is no point discussing it with the other cats. Grace regards food merely as fuel while Kate sees it as just another part of her never-ending battle to get her full emotional entitlements.

My theory that the Fluffer's a talking feline foodie gets support that very evening when Michael reports that she confronted him angrily in the kitchen as he was taking things out to start cooking. "She gave me a very indignant meow."

"Why?" I ask. "They'd had their dinner — I gave them dry food and she was eating it along with the other two."

"She'll eat dry food if she thinks there's no alternative," he says, "but when she saw me getting the chicken out of the fridge, she realised what she was missing out on and got cross."

It doesn't occur to us when the Fluffer begins to talk that she might also be developing in other ways until I walk into the kitchen one evening, laden with groceries, and something moves in the dim shadows on top of one of the alpine cupboards. I assume it's Grace, switch on the light and start unpacking the grocery bags. Then I realise Grace has come into the kitchen behind me. I look up and see a pair of golden eyes gazing down at me. I've placed the groceries on the part of the bench where she wants to jump down. "Hello, Fluffer," I say, astounded, and move the bags. She lands on the bench and with another jump is on the floor.

Two jumps to get down from the high cupboard, two jumps to get up. One jump onto the bench top — that would be easy, not much harder than leaping onto the dining table, which all the cats do without thinking — but then another jump, almost straight up, to the cupboard top. Grace has been getting on top of the high cupboards ever since we moved into the new house but we have never seen Kate up there and we never imagined that the Fluffer was capable of it, in the unlikely event she'd even want to. This is, after all, the same Fluffer who, only a short time ago, was relieved at not having to climb over the side fence at Paddington.

"So," I ask her, "what were you up to?"

Summer/Autumn

The Fluffer glances up at me, million-dollar eyes beautiful and blank, and goes off to join Grace at their food dishes. It's coming up to six o'clock, the cats' official dinner time. While I'm puzzling over her managing this feat and wondering what it means, I suspect that the Fluffer herself has forgotten that it ever happened.

What it means becomes apparent a few days later. The Fluffer is having a full scale development surge. But the change is more cognitive and behavioural than physical. She suddenly becomes assertive. She's always won the battles among the cats but now she becomes fierce and starts initiating the wars. The first time we become aware of this is early one morning when Michael intervenes because she has her paws pinned around Grace's neck. Grace is unable to move and is uttering anguished little cries. She appears to be getting strangled. "Nobody would like it, Fluffer," Michael tells her mildly as he pulls her away, "if you killed Grace."

Then, a couple of hours later, he finds Kate and Grace together on the balcony outside his office. This is surprising because ever since we moved in, this balcony has been Grace's territory. Visits from the other cats have only been tolerated when Michael and I are there, and even then Grace usually goes out of her way to snub or ignore Kate. This morning, though, Grace isn't being disdainful. She and Kate are sitting side by side. It becomes apparent they're taking refuge together from the Fluffer, who's turned into a storm trooper and is parading up and down on the stairs, looking for a fight.

Reviewing their behaviour over the past few days, Michael thinks that the other two cats registered this change in the Fluffer's personality before we did and are keeping out of her way. "She's going to be top cat," he says.

I find this hard to believe because while we're talking, I'm looking at the Fluffer, who's in one of her favourite locations. She's stretched out along the top of one of the high-backed armchairs, where she can doze, keep an eye on us while we eat or watch television, and at the same time monitor the street. Now that she's grown up, I think she's much more beautiful than she was as a kitten. She's basically what vets refer to as a "domestic shorthair" but with customised Persian features. Her face is round and her nose is flat. She does have a soft fringe of hair down her forelegs but most of the Persian-style hair is concentrated around her rear. In addition to her huge tail, she has very fluffy back legs, except that the long hair stops abruptly at the knee. The contrast between the upper and lower sections of her legs is so marked that when you see her from the rear she looks as though she's wearing a pair of frilly knickers that are in a constant state of falling down — an impression she exaggerates by performing, when she's happy or excited, a sort of reverse can-can in which she stretches her back legs out behind her and kicks them up into the air.

As I am looking at her I'm thinking how at Ron and Robin's Academy for Smart, Decorative and Unlighthearted Cats she must have topped all her classes in courses like "Cute Reclining Positions" and "How To Be Generally Gorgeous". The chair she's posing upon is a flecked beige which contrasts perfectly with her black coat. She's lying with her chin tipped forward over the rim so that her pretty

Summer/Autumn

black face forms a cute triangle while at the other end her plumy tail is draped elegantly across the chair.

Despite her sudden developmental surge, she looks exactly the same as she did a month ago: black and fluffy and beautiful. Utterly decorative. Indeed, I was just thinking how gorgeous she'd look with a gold velvet ribbon around her neck, and how I'd buy her one for Christmas, when Michael comes out with his views. I can't really imagine her as a thug princess dominating Grace and Kate, who are both older and brighter and more aggressive than she is. But I can see that if Michael is right, velvet ribbons are out. I should get her something in leather. With studs. Big ones.

As it happens both of us turn out to be right because the Fluffer becomes a dominatrix but on a part time basis. For a couple of hours, mostly just after meals, she'll be Storm Trooper Fluffer, tearing around the house, chasing the other two cats and starting battles. Grace, who will fight if she has to but is basically bored and irritated by spats and fisticuffs, soon starts dashing out of her way and ensconcing herself on the balcony rail where the Fluffer can't get at her. Kate meanwhile suffers reprisals for all the times she intimidated the Fluffer in the past. There is a great deal of growling and hissing and lots of rapid racings up to the roof.

But during the rest of the day nothing seems to have changed. The Fluffer has always been the most timid of the cats and this hasn't altered. Despite the fact that the cleaner comes every week, she's never gotten over her terror of him and his vacuum cleaner. She recognises the sound of his van in the street and immediately flies under the bed. Also, she is as affectionate as ever towards Michael and me. A minute after beating up her stepsisters, she will come tearing into our offices where she'll leap up on the backs of our chairs and put on impassioned performances of "you mother cat, me loving kitten", which involve walking along the tops of our chairs and purring rapturously while snuggling into the backs of our necks and sweeping her tail tenderly all over our faces. Nor does she show any signs of anxiety about her rapid switches from Cat Jekyll to Cat Hyde. In fact as far as we can observe, she has what might be described as the hedonist's approach to Multiple Personality Disorder: "So many more ways to enjoy being me."

Also, outside the warring hours her relationship with the other cats is unaltered. She loves to sleep on the bed with us but if the weather turns wet or cool and the other cats want to occupy the bedroom, the Fluffer takes herself off to sleep on the carpet next to the skirting board opposite our door. If I decide to intervene and make room for her on the bed, she allows herself to be picked up, stays where I've put her for a polite quarter of a minute and then returns to her previous position, where she settles down again with a look that says, "Thank you. But please don't worry. I'm really very comfortable here. In fact this is one of my very favourite stretches of skirting board."

Her new ascendancy doesn't seem to affect her position in the cats' evening window ritual. In the early summer nights, the trio like to gather together at the sitting room windows which face onto the street and watch the outside world. The first few weeks after we move, I'm so constantly worried about traffic that I only have to see a car coming down the street to immediately think, squashed Fluffer. So each time we open the sitting room windows we put up screens for the cats' protection. It soon becomes clear, though, that none of them has any desire to run out in front of a car. Instead what they want is to have the windows open so that they can take part in the nightlife of the street from a position of safety.

They do this according to a strict pecking order. Grace appears to be the designated adventurer, which means that she leaps out of the window and patrols the footpath, sniffing at odours and investigating under parked cars. Kate is the next most adventurous so she also gets out of the window, but she doesn't leave the front verandah. She surveys the street from behind the wrought iron railing fence while the Fluffer doesn't leave the house at all but stretches out on the windowsill and seems happy merely watching the other two.

Moreover, despite the Fluffer's new aggressiveness, Grace seems to be the leader in confrontations with neighbourhood cats. Hearing sounds of a fight on the roof one morning, I go off to investigate but before I get very far Grace comes hurtling down the stairs, her eyes wide and alarmed. I assume there's been a set-to with the creamy-white Siamese from up the street who must have had our roof as her private playground until our trio arrived. The other two cats are tearing down behind Grace. It's clear the home side has lost. I stop myself from grinning and saying in disbelief, "The Siamese took on the three of you and won!" because they all look so upset.

Grace's manner conveys shame, fear, defeat. Kate, who is in the rear, also looks very frightened and anxious. Even as she and Grace are running away, I can see them processing the awful implications of their setback. What's going to happen now? What does it mean for their overall defence strategy? How are their regional interests going to be affected? Who, in short, is the creamy Siamese going to saunter off to now with the report that the new neighbours on the corner of the lane are a bunch of wusses? But it's the Fluffer, in the middle, whose reaction I notice most sharply. She's tearing down behind Grace. Her eyes are huge with fright and she's charging along with the rest of them but at the same time I have the distinct feeling that she doesn't really know what is happening.

Very shortly after this incident, the Fluffer suddenly demonstrates a new skill. She discovers manual dexterity. When the cats are jostling for positions around the food dishes, Grace has long known how to gain an advantage. As the cats lower their heads to one bowl, then raise them again quickly to inspect another that looks more promising, Grace is the only one who's understood that cats don't necessarily have to approach bowls. Bowls can also be made to approach cats. So as Kate and the Fluffer attempt to converge on a bowl, Grace wins out by simply stretching a paw between them and drawing the bowl towards her.

The other cats don't resist this manoeuvre. They clearly regard it as one of those mysterious events in the universe that are beyond their comprehension. Until the morning when Grace reaches out her paw as usual to draw a bowl towards her and the Fluffer stops her by simply butting the extended paw out of the way with her shoulder. After which she takes over the bowl. An hour later, in the middle of a wrestle, she makes the equally interesting discovery that she can control Kate, who's the only one of the them with a collar, by hooking a paw around the collar and pulling.

However, some things are clearly beyond her new skills. As part of her development surge she becomes much more interested in hunting, but unlike Grace, who's been studying the local prey ever since we moved in and knows what's feasible, the Fluffer hasn't had a learning period. She goes from pursuing the tiny midges that gather over the fruit bowl on hot summer afternoons to aspiring to the biggest catch in the neighbourhood. I come across her sitting on the bedroom windowsill and uttering little hunting cries while her eyes are fixed on the large black and white magpies that swoop backwards and forwards in the sky above the house.

The windowsill is about fifteen feet above the ground, but the magpies must be several times that distance above us.

"I think they're out of your league, Fluffer," I say.

She doesn't look at me, but stretches her neck, her eyes intent, and gives another little cry. One of the magpies has flown lower, dipping down towards the lane. I suspect it hasn't noticed the Fluffer sitting there, following its every movement with all her predator's instincts on high boil. But even if it has, I doubt it would be concerned. In a contest between it and the Fluffer, my money would be on the bird.

"You need what the military call enhancements, Fluffer," I explain. "Teeth and claws and being able to jump aren't going to get you within cooee of one of these big critters."

I have only the most basic knowledge of military equipment but I review it rapidly for her benefit — guns, tanks, planes with bombs, grenades... Then I have an inspiration.

"What about a ground-to-air missile, Fluffer?" I say. "We'll get Ron to bring you one back from the States for Christmas."

I can imagine her being very happy on the wide window ledge, with a bandana around her forehead and her own little missile installation. Bringing down bird after bird.

KINKY AND DIVERSE

One of the advantages of our cat-sharing arrangement is that we can blame the co-owners (or previous owners, in Kate's case) for their inadequacies. Although by the end of their first year Grace and the Fluffer have spent more than half their lives with us, as we see it Ron and Robin raised them through a critical period of their kittenhood and can therefore be held responsible for major personality flaws which Grace and the Fluffer start displaying as adults and which Kate — because of her passion for emulating — also exhibits.

As we approach the end of our first year, it begins to strike me that while Ron and Robin's criteria for their perfect cat have been met — though it's true that they were wanting affectionate, intelligent cats rather than *an* affectionate cat and *an* intelligent cat — I haven't been so lucky. I can recall, after Pusscat died, looking forward to a cat who'd have soft, silver-grey fur and a beautiful face with markings a little reminiscent of a tiger's, who would be sociable and affectionate, who'd purr on my lap while I watched TV and sleep on my bed in winter and would be particularly fond of dinner parties during which it would station itself next to a susceptible guest who'd feed it tidbits.

Well, all the cats have beautiful faces and Kate has some tiger-style markings. None of them has silver-grey fur but the Fluffer's black coat is a perfectly adequate substitute and I also love Grace and Kate's multicoloured coats. In addition, they are all affectionate, but they've conspicuously failed to meet some of the other job requirements. They're not sociable. They don't like dinner parties. And they positively hate sitting on laps.

In fact Michael and I are discovering to our disappointment, that Grace, Kate and the Fluffer are social failures. I don't feel this could be in any way our fault because, as I've said earlier, all my previous cats were gregarious. While I suspect that both Pusscat and GB privately regarded social occasions as useful opportunities to audition possible new owners, they were always enthusiastic about having visitors. Pusscat used to consider it her duty to charm every arrival to the house. Sometimes she succeeded so well that we had people to dinner who spent the entire night communing with her, which could get a bit boring for us, but at least it meant our guests were having a good time.

Despite the shortness of his stay with us, GB also did his utmost. He used to sit serenely beside us when we had company and radiate such well-mannered charm you were sure he was saying, "It's really extremely pleasant to have you with us. A glass of champagne, perhaps? How

Summer/Autumn

about some smoked salmon? Oh, is that piece for me? Really? How thoughtful of you."

By contrast, Grace, Kate and the Fluffer don't even seem to have heard of working the room. As kittens, all three used to be sociable and would accept pats from visitors and peer up at newcomers with eager curiosity. Now the whole business of people coming to the house — strange voices, unfamiliar odours and changes to routines — seems to agitate them. The Fluffer, whose looks and charm we want to show off, disappears under our bed. Grace gives the newcomers a glance and immediately leaves the room. "She's the intelligent one," we find ourselves saying helplessly to visitors who only get to admire the flick of her elegant tail as she goes out the door.

Even Kate, who's always eager for attention, doesn't like company. Although since Robin came for her two-week stay, she seems to have decided it would be wise to be friendly towards any single women who visit the house when I'm out. Presumably she suspects that any one of them might turn out to be a permanent Thea replacement and she is operating on the sensible political principle that it's never too early to ingratiate yourself with a new regime. Various women coming to see Michael on business have therefore been the recipients of her very affectionate attentions, complete with significant eye contact and coaxing paws upon their knees. While Michael claims he's done everything possible to reassure Kate that I'm not being phased out, she never seems to believe him. He also says she always looks immensely relieved when I reappear. But I think this is just a manoeuvre (on both their parts) to keep in my good books.

There are exceptions to this general dislike of company. All the cats appear to approve of single visitors who stay the night. Indeed, they seem to consider it positively inhospitable not to sleep with them. And the Fluffer will join company if there's nice food on offer, but it takes a lot of coaxing. She has to have her own chair. She won't purr. She stares at the food as if her eyes can somehow channel it up off the plate and will throw tantrums in the kitchen if there are delays about giving her the leftovers.

I'm particularly upset by the cats' refusal to sit on laps as I like having a cat on my knee at night when I'm watching TV and feel that with three cats in the house, at least one of them ought to be amenable to sitting on my lap. My late Pusscat was so fond of taking an evening nap on a knee in front of the television that on nights when neither of us watched it she'd stalk around the house with a "What's up with you people?" look on her face. GB leapt up on Michael's lap the first time he came to call and seemed to regard knee-sitting as an integral part of cat—human communication.

By contrast Kate, who used to sit on my knee when she was little, now starts to growl when I try to hold her on my lap while the Fluffer doesn't seem to have gotten her mind around the "sitting" part. She keeps trying to stand up on her back legs so that I find I'm holding her awkwardly against my chest while she wriggles and apparently tries to work out how she can escape over my shoulder. As for Grace, the one time I tried it she was very polite but clearly thought I was demented and sat on my knee in a manner reminiscent of a passenger whose aeroplane is being hijacked.

Compared to these deficiencies, the cats' other common character flaw is minor, though occasionally embarrassing: they all have psycho-sexual kinks. Kate has never gotten over her fondness for escorting people to the bathroom. To our visitors' surprise, they will suddenly become aware that the door has quietly opened and their every move is being scrutinised by a large and serious pair of hazel eyes.

This whole problem wouldn't exist if it was impossible for her get into the bathroom but, as we soon discover, visitors generally don't consider it good manners to make an effort to close the bathroom door. They just gently tap it shut behind them, which means the lock doesn't close properly. All Kate has to do is jump against the lower part of the door and it rebounds. We could say, "Please close the bathroom door firmly behind you," except that makes it sound as though we're excessively selfconscious about bodily functions. (I did think of putting up a notice saying "Please lock door. Voyeur cat in residence" until I realised it would probably have the opposite effect.)

At the same time it's become apparent that our dear, admirable, intelligent Grace has quite a thing about women's underwear. This gets to be public knowledge in embarrassing circumstances when a visitor discovers her in the process of dragging my one silky nightdress across the floor.

The Fluffer's problem is rather more complicated. She's been injudicious in her choice of a name. Well, strictly speaking, we've been injudicious in choosing her name, but we see it as her fault because it wasn't as though we'd ever set out to christen her "The Fluffer", she just earned it by engaging in excessive amounts of fluffiness in the line of duty.

What happens is that one night Michael reports to me that the manager of the local bottle shop has overheard us talking about "the Fluffer" and has later informed Michael that, in Mexican brothels, a fluffer is a prostitute who gets the men excited.

"Oh," I say. "Really?"

It has never occurred to me that there might be such a need for this role in brothels that the job has its own specific designation. I'm a bit taken aback that we've inadvertently called our cat after a type of sex worker, but then decide that we're not likely to meet many people familiar with the division of labour in Mexican brothels. Also, it would be too hard to change the Fluffer's name now because she knows it, and she will turn her head towards us when we say it.

By summer, though, things have become dramatically worse. We discover the term "fluffer" is very well established throughout the North American porn film industry and is now starting to become common knowledge. I begin to think seriously about a change of name.

"Perhaps we should start calling her Olive," I say to Michael. "She's heard Ron and Robin call her that."

"Olive," I say warmly to the Fluffer next time I see her. "Here, kitty, here, Olive."

I try to sound convincing but all my performance clearly doesn't impress the Fluffer. She seems to feel that something odd is going on. She looks at me, looks away, and then does what any sensible cat does when faced with an awkward moment — she occupies herself with a long and intensive wash.

Summer/Autumn

Michael is amused by the situation, I'm not. I can foresee years of explaining ahead. But then I decide that as we can't change her name, we might as well go for a print-the-legend type approach. All that's required are some adjustments to the story of how we got the cats. I can imagine myself saying, "We adopted Kate and Grace through a vet but the Fluffer belonged to a brothel down the road. That's how she got her name. The building got sold and they couldn't take her with them when they moved."

I have no doubt that most people will find this story believable. As many cat advice books will earnestly inform you, mother cats train their kittens to urinate and use their bowels by licking their bottoms. So kittens standardly present their rear ends to their mothers, but grow out of the behaviour as they mature. At least cats are said to grow out of it, and Grace and Kate certainly have. But not the Fluffer. She seems to assume that people will be as happy to see one end of her as the other and proudly presents her face and her backside pretty much as if they are interchangeable. As a result, a number of relatively infrequent visitors to the house could effortlessly identify her rear view in a police line-up.

What exactly the cats' co-owners can be expected to do about these character deficiencies I'm not sure, but as mid-December and the time for Ron and Robin's return approaches, I cheer myself up against the prospect of the trio's departure by telling them that I expect them to come back to us in February as perfectly behaved cats. No sharpening of claws on every surface within reach. No outbreaks of ritualised violence between six and seven in the morning. No systematic dispersals of insect carcasses in the front hall. No abductions of socks from the clothesline. No loungings on top of the fax machine. No excursions into the kitchen cupboards. No leaving of muddy footprints on windowsills. No chewing of newspapers, no depositing of feathers, no excavating of pot plants, no souveniring of plastic lids... The list of practices I want the co-owners to delete from the cats' lifestyles is approaching the high three figures when Michael appears with the news that Ron and Robin's house is still not habitable.

"They are coming back, but they're going to move into a flat for the first few weeks. They hope to move into their house after Christmas."

"What should we do?" I ask, thinking that the cats will only have been in the new house for a bit over a month. Then they'll be in the flat for three weeks. Then Ron and Robin's house for three weeks. Then back to us.

"They want to take them, but they don't think it's fair for them to be moved so much. And I don't either," he adds firmly.

I say yes while thinking to myself, no herb garden this summer. I'd been intending to plant it while the cats were at Ron and Robin's. None of the trio has a high regard for the rights of other living things and can't see why anything so inconsequential as a bunch of parsley seedlings should come between them and their natural urge to dig a really nice big hole in a freshly filled pot. I know that if I try to start a herb garden while they are in residence, I'll find all the little plants dug up and crushed within hours of putting them in their pots.

Instead of taking the cats, the co-owners come to dinner

Summer/Autumn

bearing what looks like enough food to keep three normal cats going for a decade and Grace for a couple of weeks. Kate and the Fluffer react initially as they do to most visitors. Kate runs up to the roof. The Fluffer hides under the bed. Grace comes forward to welcome Robin but doesn't seem to recognise Ron. It is two months since she saw Robin but nearly five months since she last saw him. She accepts pats from the co-owners with her usual graciousness and seems to stay around us more than usual while we are having drinks on the roof before dinner, but then during dinner she appears in the dining room and, without a glance at the table of guests who have all turned to look at her, she goes up to the wall, pauses by the skirting board, and pisses.

The world turns out to be full of cat psychologists. Everyone to whom I tell the story of Grace's behaviour has a different interpretation of the incident. As she has never done such a thing before, I'd just assumed she was very upset. She felt a connection with Ron and Robin but couldn't make sense of what was happening. However, this analysis gets generally dismissed as far too simple. I'm told instead that she knows exactly who Ron and Robin are and was trying to let them know that this is her house now and she doesn't want to leave. I'm told that she's angry with them, firstly for going away and then for coming back, because she now sees them as a threat to her re-established stability. And I'm told it's revenge — she was literally showing Ron and Robin what she thinks of them.

What impresses me most, though, about these explanations is the speed with which people are able to provide them. Almost before I have finished my brief account of the incident, the person to whom I'm talking is nodding their head and coming forward with a detailed interpretation. It suddenly occurs to me that while I spend much of my time preoccupied with what I'm writing, a lot of the rest of the community are equally busy analysing their pets.

My cat psychologists don't have particular advice about how to respond to Grace's outburst. Michael and I do what seems obvious — mop up the mess and act as if nothing unusual has happened while trying to be affectionate and reassuring. Once the moment's passed, Grace seems to be her normal self again. The catastrophe that could have affected her appetite doesn't appear to exist and there are no repeats of the outburst on the co-owners' later visits. But the incident makes me even more anxious and selfconscious in my dealings with her. The feeling I had about her at the time of Kate's arrival, when I said to Michael that she didn't think she was a cat, becomes stronger.

Indeed, one of my problems with Grace is that she doesn't put me in mind of a cat. I can see that she's very elegant and distinctive but her appearance is unfamiliar. There were no Burmese or Siamese, or even part-Burmese or part-Siamese, cats around when I was growing up. By contrast, every time I look at Kate, she evokes memories of a lifetime of cats. Childhood cats sitting on farm fences; next door cats (always soundly fed but invariably hungry) visiting student households; neighbourhood cats setting up arrangements with me when I was living on my own. Even the odd half-broken thrum that develops in her purr seems exactly what a cat should have.

Summer/Autumn

But when I think about Grace's appearance, the first thing I remember is that morning, just after we moved house, when we were on the roof together and she quailed at the swooping magpie. It struck me then how bird-like she herself is with her narrow head, pointed face, slender limbs and elongated tail. But not a modern bird, an evolutionary bird, still emerging from being a reptile with wings. After that I call her, "My pterodactyl."

I'm aware, though, that unfamiliarity doesn't entirely explain my feelings. I've never had any previous acquaintance with a cat like the Fluffer and yet I never have the same anxiety about her. When she does one of her sudden switches from peaceable, affectionate cat to thug princess, I just say, "Oh, the Fluffer's having one of her adrenalin surges," as if I'd always lived with cats who were a'tiskett a'taskett, a kitten in a basket cats one minute and gun-totin' psychopaths the next. (Admittedly there's good reason for not taking the Fluffer's reigns of terror too seriously. We discover after a couple of weeks that when she starts chasing the other cats, all we have to do is pick her up and put her in a room on her own. Whereupon she forgets the whole thing, has a wash and goes to sleep.)

Much less dramatic contrasts in Grace's behaviour continue to worry me though; and her many talents and achievements only make me feel even more inadequate. Every time Michael proudly describes some new skill or grasp of concept that she's displayed, I get the feeling once again that I'm not cut out to be even the quarter part-owner of a gifted cat. I'm aware that despite how fond I am of her, the underlying problem is that I've never really bonded with her as I have with the other cats. What makes it worse is that I think she knows.

This isn't just me being hypersensitive. Grace has always been much more aware than the other two cats of human moods. When she was still quite a small kitten and I got some bad news, I noticed that she stayed around me all that day and Michael has observed her doing the same thing when he's been anxious. (There's a downside to this. As Michael says, it's bad enough being depressed without feeling you have to keep up appearances in front of the cat.)

One evening just after we move house, I give what must have been a realistic-sounding whimper as I'm tiredly climbing the stairs and then find Grace is waiting for me on the top landing, peering up at me with concern. I'm so surprised and amused at her sympathy that I can't help giving another whimper. "She's taking a lean on you, Grace," observes Michael disapprovingly. The second whimper clearly doesn't sound as convincing as the first because she gives me a doubtful look and walks away.

Also, if it's true that cats can only envisage themselves in two types of relationships — either as kittens or as mother cats — it's clear that Grace sees herself as an adult and a caregiver and regards Kate and the Fluffer as kittens. The difference shows up sharply in their daily routines. Grace goes about on her own while Kate and the Fluffer mostly want to be around Michael and me. The standard scenario is for Kate and the Fluffer to be sitting in the foreground, waiting expectantly for whatever is about to happen, and for Grace to be in the background, also watching and waiting but contriving to make it appear as though she just happened to be passing by at that particular moment

Summer/Autumn

and thought she would sit down and give her left paw a quick wash. We can tell when she's worried that something is seriously amiss — if, for example, we've been away much longer than usual — because she will be positioned up closer to the other cats.

Similarly, if we are watching television Kate and the Fluffer will always come in to see us, while Grace rarely does unless she has a reason — she's had a shock of some sort and wants reassurance, or she's anxious. As a result, a visit from Grace is a bit like a combination of a royal visit and a military tour of inspection. We feel partly honoured by her appearance and partly as though she's arrived to check on proceedings and reassure herself that everything's in order. There's always a strong hint in her manner that we can't be relied on and need to be kept under constant surveillance.

The most marked example of her adult role is with the Fluffer. We had always felt that she protected the Fluffer but never had any real evidence of this until one hot afternoon when we're all sitting on the front balcony in the shade of the big tree. When we first saw the house we thought that this tree was one of its major attractions. We were sure that Grace would love it. We could see her climbing up it, leaping onto it from the first floor balcony and exploring it as enthusiastically as she'd climbed all over the other much smaller trees in our old neighbourhood.

But the big tree is deceptive. There are masses of branches but the outlying ones are too slender and elastic even for Grace's slight weight, so she can't jump onto the tree from the balcony. At the same time she can't scramble up the trunk until a wire screen around the base gets removed. Meanwhile every instinct she's got is telling her, "It's a tree. Climb it." She eyes it beadily from all directions. While we sit and sip our drinks, she stalks up and down the balcony railing, staring at the tree. Then it occurs to her that she may be able to leap onto a branch from the neighbour's balcony and she sets off to climb around to the adjoining balcony to try from this new vantage point.

The other two cats watch her. At one stage Kate leaps up onto the balcony rail to join in the adventure. Grace, irritated, turns her back on her. Kate jumps back onto the ground and pretends the whole incident hasn't happened. The Fluffer gets a different treatment. When she starts scrambling up the wrought iron fence to join Grace, who's poised on the railing studying how to climb around the end of the balcony, Grace simply leans over and with her paw pushes on the Fluffer's head to discourage her. The Fluffer climbs down again.

Michael and I stare, astonished and impressed. Ever since the days when she fell off cushions, we have known what poor balance the Fluffer has. We get nervous when she attempts tasks like walking along the balcony railing, which are easy enough for cats of ordinary competence like Kate and effortless for brilliant ones like Grace. But we'd never realised before that Grace also knows the Fluffer's limits.

This isn't a random event. On several occasions we see Grace put out a paw to stop the Fluffer following her out of the house. We also learn that Grace can distinguish between the Fluffer's normal daily fits of madness and when she's being, so to speak, mad north-by-northwest. I become aware of this for the first time when I go into the dining room just as it's becoming dark one evening and find Grace and the Fluffer sitting on the table. I say, "No!" loudly in irritation. There's a state of constant war between me and Grace about the dining room table. She likes to sit on it because it's comfortable and also the best vantage point for monitoring the sitting room. I don't like her to sit on it because it's unhygienic and I don't want cats' hair in my food. Both cats immediately leap off and it's only then that I register how oddly they were sitting. They were side by side and Grace had her teeth in the scruff of the Fluffer's neck and was holding her down with a paw.

I soon see why. The Fluffer is having one of those episodes that most cats seem to go through occasionally when they tear wildly around the house. I have read explanations of these fits in the cat advice books and know from experience that they pass of their own accord but I feel silly when I realise that I interrupted Grace when she was trying to calm the Fluffer down.

I decide that even if the Fluffer's fit will pass of its own accord, Grace — as a cat — probably knows what should be done better than any human being. If she was taking action to calm the Fluffer, then that's the right thing to do. After all, I've seen Grace herself in one of these moods. Perhaps they're awful to experience — much more frightening for the cat undergoing them than human observers realise. Or maybe they're dangerous — a cat in a mad mood is vulnerable to attack or could do itself some real damage. I give her an apologetic look,

The Cat Who Looked at the Sky

say, "Sorry, Grace," and go in pursuit of the Fluffer, who has now leapt onto the mantelpiece and is staring with wild eyes about the room. I tell myself that if I've stopped Grace playing mother cat, then I have to take on the responsibility.

I seize the Fluffer and carry her, struggling, to an armchair where I sit down and hold her firmly on my lap while gripping her by the back of the neck. I release my grip after about ten minutes and she tries to do a lunge off my knees, so I grasp her neck again. I don't talk to her or pay her any particular attention but I hold her with one hand and keep the other around her in imitation of a gesture I remember very clearly, half-restraint, half-embrace. After a time she starts to relax and begins to stretch out. I still keep a firm hold on her neck but stroke her gently. A few minutes later, I let her go. She begins to wash in preparation for her nap.

I can remember the gesture of half-embrace, half-restraint because it's one I have seen the Fluffer do herself. One day when Kate was giving the Fluffer one of her head-washings that inevitably degenerate into biting sessions, I saw the Fluffer stretch out a paw just as Kate was about to bite her. The Fluffer placed her paw across Kate's shoulders. Kate immediately stopped what she was doing and settled down to go to sleep. The Fluffer closed her eyes. Half a minute later they were both sound asleep, side by side, with the Fluffer's paw still holding Kate.

All the time I spend thinking about my relationship with Grace doesn't help me resolve the issue, though. I mostly end up remembering the cat experts who say that all relationships, whether human or animal, are the same. They can't be built on good intentions. It's fate, timing, chemistry. I remember how quickly I fell for Kate and think sadly that perhaps I'm predisposed to needy, pretty, not-very-bright tabbies. Finally I decide there's nothing for it but to be philosophical. Grace is not short of people who love her unreservedly. If it was a matter of choice, I'd be amongst them. Instead I remind myself of all the things that we have done with the cats that have turned out to be right.

Chief amongst these was the decision to keep the cats with us instead of sending them to Ron and Robin's at Christmas. Afterwards it becomes apparent that it takes the whole summer for all three cats to become fully confident in their new environment. When I look back on this process I realise they colonised our new house in stages. For the first few weeks they mostly occupied the combined sitting/dining room. They would go into other rooms in the house — they'd haunt the kitchen at meal times and would visit our bedroom and offices to see what we were doing — but they'd always sleep in the sitting room. Later on the sleeping zone was extended to include the stairs and landings around our offices. Then they started establishing favourite sleeping spots throughout the house. Grace naps in a chair on the front balcony and the Fluffer finds a nook on the landing at the top of the stairs while Kate the Emulator occupies whichever spot one of the others has just ceased patronising.

They take over the roof garden in a similar way. In our first weeks in the house they prefer to visit it in human company. When I go up there to tend the plants, I find they usually all come up after me, so that I get into the habit of calling to them to join me. Then they start to go up on their own after breakfast, presumably as part of checking their territory, and they start to include it in their games. Then the visits become more frequent until, after a month, I find they're often sitting up there during the day and it becomes obvious that they feel as secure about being there as they do in the house itself, even though there's a risk of other cats visiting and of magpies swooping on them from above.

Of course colonising the new neighbourhood's more complicated. Surry Hills is one of those areas that social commentators call "diverse" and the cats are as diverse as the human residents. Up the end of our cul-de-sac there's a couple of dolorous-looking tomcats who date back to the days of pre-diversity when the neighbourhood more commonly got described as "down and out". This duo take one look at Grace, who is naturally the first to venture out onto the street, and raise their eyebrows at each other,

"Just what we need. Another desexed, uppity part Burmese who's got tickets on herself because she was adopted through a vet. I'll bet she's never even met a cat without a microchip before. Let's just mosey on down and acquaint her with the fact that all this gentrification shit don't apply to us."

Fortunately, between her kittenhood in Rozelle and her young adult days in Paddington, Grace seems to have acquired enough street savvy to ease her way into her new environment. The dolorous-looking toms sit on their stretches of footpath and eye her as she scampers about, so that Michael says worriedly to her, "One day, Grace, one of those toms is really going to go for you."

Yet nothing happens. She appears to know how to avoid trouble. There are a few nights when we hear growls and screams outside and Grace comes flying through the sitting room windows so rapidly that all we see is a flash of brown and black. But she doesn't get into any serious wars, for we never see any marks about her neck or ears. And one night, as the street lamps are coming on, we even see her playing a game with a graceful black and white female who lives down the street. The pair chase each other through some leafy undergrowth on a nature strip, dashing their paws at the long overhanging summer grass and leaping in and out of the gutter as they romp.

In all the best class wars it seems you're most hated by the group with whom you have the most in common. Accordingly, the expensive pedigreed cats who've only moved into the area in the last few years despise our cats even more than do the long term semi-ferals. These gilt-edged recent arrivals collectively turn up their properly bred noses at our three. The creamy Siamese who was accustomed to queening it over our roof garden before our trio arrived, gives Grace, Kate and the Fluffer scornful glances and we can hear her saying, "Well, their backgrounds are very — you know — diverse. I heard that one was dumped while the other two got selected out of a barrel of foundlings at a vet's. You'd wonder, wouldn't you, why people bother. I mean, they can't fend for themselves like proper ferals and yet they don't have pedigrees. All I can say is that I'm glad they can't have kittens."

While Grace gets to know the neighbourhood within a month, it takes all summer for Kate and the Fluffer to start exploring, and even then I suspect that Kate isn't really all that keen on the idea. She goes outdoors more because it's the sort of thing that a cat is supposed to do rather than because she's curious about her surroundings.

The Fluffer, by contrast, becomes adventurous as part of her general developmental surge. By late summer she's disappearing some evenings for hours. Grace stops trying to prevent her leaving the house but she lets it be known that if the Fluffer wants to go exploring, she'll have to bear the consequences. One night when all three cats are out on the street there's suddenly the sound of a wild brawl. A second later Grace comes flying through the window with Kate half a minute behind her. Michael and I look at each other, at the window, then at the cats.

"Where's the Fluffer then?" we ask. "Have you two left her out there on her own?"

Grace has sat down and started to wash. She has a wonderful way of holding up her neat black paw in an elegant curve for her tongue's inspection which makes it look as though she's wearing evening gloves. She doesn't raise her eyes from this important business. The message is clear. She's learnt to survive on the streets through the exercise of care and caution. She's very observant, she gets out before there's trouble and she has no intention of becoming involved in heroics on behalf of her younger sister. If the Fluffer wants to be a big cat and go out and have serious cat adventures, she'll have to learn to fight her own battles. We get up to investigate but the street's now quiet and empty. A few minutes later, to my intense relief, the Fluffer comes in the window. Grace and Kate show not the slightest interest in her arrival.

"Learn to keep up with the others next time," Michael advises her.

NEW STERN REGIME

Some time around Christmas, Kate develops a new feature. It seems to appear one day of its own accord. I'm following her down the stairs when I suddenly notice how substantial she's become across her rear.

"That's quite a behind you have there, Kate," I say to her, impressed.

I'm impressed because the only word to describe Kate's bottom is "authoritative". This is clearly the bottom she was meant to have. It's large and round and firm and generous. It showcases her elaborate markings and seems designed for motherhood. In fact I immediately imagine her lying on her side, her bottom facing towards me and a tumble of kittens playing over it while Kate gazes proudly at me over their heads. I find myself sighing a little. One of my and Michael's occasional "what if/what might have been" type conversations is about what sorts of mothers the three cats would have made. We always

Summer/Autumn

end up agreeing that of the trio, it was Kate who should have had kittens.

We think that Grace would be a perfect mother but so anxious she would be permanently stressed. With her nervy intelligence she'd be terrified that whenever a kitten took a step beyond her reach, it was about to do itself mortal damage, and she'd spend her time anticipating dangers unlikely to befall even the most accident-prone offspring. The Fluffer would be quite the opposite. She'd go through the experience in a manner so sweetly unfocused you wouldn't be sure she had actually noticed anything was happening. She'd be a competent mother but so dreamy and not-quite-there in her usual way that after a couple of weeks we would realise we were not the only ones becoming unnerved by her manner. I could see us coming downstairs one morning and discovering that while the Fluffer was still feeding her kittens, the task of raising them was now being carried out collaboratively by Kate and Grace.

Kate, by contrast, would rear her family with a textbook type perfection. Her kittens mightn't be the sanest or the brightest on the block but they'd definitely be the best brought up. All her emotional intensity would go into ensuring that she got exactly right the maternal mix of delivering affection, providing protection, developing skills and promoting independence. Indeed, the only thing we could see her doing wrong was deciding in a determined and utterly Kate-like way that she could do it even better with a few more kittens and going out and appropriating some other cat's progeny.

The Cat Who Looked at the Sky

After Kate's growth surge, I begin to wonder if the Fluffer is going to go through a similar late expansion and start to watch her more closely. While doing so I remember how once when she was a tiny kitten I saw her butting Grace out of her way to get to the food bowls and thought that when she grew up, she'd be one of those large, phlegmatic-looking black cats who always appear to be either asleep or just about to nod off. Instead, a year later, she's still a little cat beneath all her fur and anyone seeing Kate and her together would quite reasonably assume that they were a mother and her near-adult kitten. The Fluffer does, however, have very large front paws — almost as large as Kate's — so that I keep thinking it's possible that at some point, the rest of her body is going to follow suit.

However the only change I observe is that the Fluffer has taken to sitting up. Once she always hunched down on her forequarters. Now I often find her sitting with her head held high and her plumy tail draped in front of her with painterly elegance, as if she's practising her pose for when Sir Joshua Reynolds comes by later to do her portrait.

"Well, Fluffer," I say, giving her a stroke under the chin, "you're really a high society cat, aren't you? You'd live on lobster, caviar and smoked salmon if we could afford it, and your photo would be constantly in *Vogue*."

The Fluffer responds to my caress by standing up and rubbing her head against me while arching her back and tail upwards in delight. She now has her life neatly timetabled. For two hours a day she's a gourmet cat, for another hour she is a psychopath, and in between she's her usual affectionate self.

By this time all of the in-house violence has become quite organised. Grace and Kate have settled into a sort of accommodation where they tend, like teenage siblings, to have short frequent squabbles. Grace, unsurprisingly, is bad-tempered before breakfast and will often turn on Kate as they're heading towards their food bowls. She will lash out at Kate or try to trip her up or just be generally malicious. One morning I notice Kate's snowy whiskers peeking out of the front of the covered litter tray at the same time that Grace does. Grace, whose own whiskers are nothing to write home about, stalks over and gives Kate a completely unprovoked swipe across the face. (It's hard not to feel jealousy was involved.) The Fluffer doesn't participate in these pre-breakfast scuffles but gets transformed into Mr Hyde once she's eaten. She chases Grace and Kate up the stairs and once she starts to become aggressive, the other cats react.

The result is a series of mad chases up and down the double staircase with periodic sounds of battle as each cat flees from or pursues one or both of the others, except that in some sort of hangover from her role as mother figure to the little black cat, Grace never chases the Fluffer. She retaliates if the Fluffer attacks her, but she never chases her. This forbearance doesn't win her any favours. Every few days, the Fluffer grabs or bites Grace so fiercely that she cries out in pain.

While it improves her performance in other areas, we soon discover that maturity doesn't do anything for either the Fluffer's sense of balance or her grasp of gravity. She still misjudges distances and falls off places that the other cats negotiate without difficulty. Also, if she doesn't get things when she's coming, she tends to get them when she's going. Her huge fluffy tail held happily aloft is wonderful for disconnecting electrical cords and swiping vulnerable objects off the tops of low tables.

"You're a bad, depraved, lamentable pussycat," I tell her at the end of a week when she's taken out the iron, broken two stems of buds off the orchid and is wanted for questioning about her role in the disappearance of my favourite hair clip.

"I'm a nice cat," says the Fluffer firmly. She hasn't got much of a vocabulary but she knows what she thinks.

"Tell that to Grace next time you're strangling her," I answer, but then reflect that while Grace is good at recognising our moods, the Fluffer's more directly concerned with trying to make us happy. For example, she's a great practitioner of what I call "supportive sleeping". As with Grace and Kate, she has her favourite places for naps but if I'm engaged in a task for a long time — if I'm gardening or painting a wall — she'll come to where I am, position herself in a spot close by so she can see me, and then go to sleep. During a big job, the Fluffer will log up five to six hours of steady supportive sleep and if I move, she'll get up, reorient herself in a new position from which she can see me, and resume her sleep.

And it's the Fluffer, alone among the cats, who decides one evening to sit on my lap. She simply leaps up onto my knee and arranges herself comfortably as though she's been doing it for years. Not that we regard this gesture as being entirely motivated by affection — the weather is becoming cooler. The Fluffer is always quicker than the other cats at identifying new sources of comfort. She is the first to realise when the heater has been turned on and drapes herself across the arm of the sofa facing it. (I once read a description of what it was like to come by ship from the icy air of the north into the warmth of the Caribbean and ever afterwards when I see the Fluffer with her face tipped up to enjoy the heater, I think of her as a cat on a boat sailing out of New England into the balmy air of the south.)

This new lap-sitting development immediately attracts Kate's interest. For several weeks, from her current position on a dining chair, she watches as the Fluffer comes in, jumps up onto my lap and proceeds to go to sleep until finally one night, when the Fluffer's out of the room, she decides to try it for herself.

'Hello, Katie Kate,' I say, giving her a stroke.

She sits down rather tensely and it soon becomes apparent the situation is not working for either of us. She doesn't seem to realise that the purpose of the exercise is to relax and go to sleep. Instead she sits upright with her head held high and all her weight resting heavily on one of my legs. It's as though on my lap is famously precarious and cats keep falling off it to their doom. Eventually, to my relief, she gets down and walks away. She looks exactly like some member of the public who's sampled the city's latest fashionable cafe and been unimpressed. The expression on her face says very clearly, "Well, I suppose some cats must like it but I sure as hell think it's overrated."

I say to Michael, "Thank heavens for the Fluffer. She's the only one of these cats who's relaxing."

He raises his eyebrows expressively. We are having one of our periods of feeling overwhelmed by the cats. In contrast to all those times when they're comforting or relaxing or entertaining, to all the afternoons when Michael greets me on my return from work with an anecdote which begins, "The cats are so funny …", there are times when they drive us crazy.

Each cat starts out by practising one of its specialties. Grace harasses us nonstop for food. Kate chews up important bits of paper. The Fluffer spreads fur all over the clean washing. This raises the emotional temperature. A cat gets snapped at, which upsets all three of them. But instead of quietly retiring until we've recovered our equilibriums, they become what Michael calls "clingy". With a great air of drama and self-importance they'll escort us wherever we go in the house — one cat in the vanguard, one underfoot and the other in the rear — or they'll hang around and engage in heavy body language, and having the three of them all simultaneously rubbing their cheeks up and down on the nearest bits of furniture always makes me feel like I'm in the middle of an overwrought mime performance.

Michael suffers more from this onslaught of cats than I do because he does the cooking. One of the key principles of modern domestic architecture seems to be that kitchens do not have doors and a typical episode of feline overwhelmingness begins with a dispute about food. Michael arrives in the kitchen to start cooking and finds himself immediately joined by three cats who all stare at him.

"You've been fed," he tells them. "Thea says she fed you half an hour ago."

Expressions of surprise and consternation on all three faces. "Fed? We don't think so. We'd remember."

He goes to their bowls to check, followed by the trio. "I can see the fresh food in your dishes!"

The three cats glance briefly at their dishes and then back at him. The looks on their faces at this point always remind me of the Richard Pryor joke about the man whose wife comes home to find him in bed with another woman. "Who're you gonna believe? Me — or your own lyin' eyes?"

By the time I arrive in the kitchen the cats will be gathered together in the middle of the floor. All three will be on high alert, heads up, eyes big, tails prominent, and their poses will emphasise the contrast in their appearances — Kate, large and round with perfect grey-brown markings; the Fluffer, small and black and furry with expressive golden eyes; and Grace, black and tan with elegant head and eloquent tail. They'll look like a painting called 'Cats of the World' (detail). They'll also have arranged themselves so as to impede Michael as much as possible. He has to skirt carefully around them to get to either the fridge, the sink or the stove. With perfect timing, they converge on him at exactly the moment when he can't stop preparations to capture cat number one, carry her from the room, lock her in another room, return to the kitchen, repeat operation with cat number two, ditto cat three, then wash his hands carefully and resume cooking.

On one such occasion I say to him, "Do you remember our plan to have two cats part time?"

"It all seemed so rational," he says wistfully.

I nod, remembering how I used to feel rather proud of us. It was all going to be so simple, so undemanding, such a suitable arrangement for all six participants. I recall my two imaginary black and white kittens who were going to curl up and sleep decoratively on chairs together in between sessions of washing each others' ears. They'd be grown up by now and I know exactly what they would be like. They'd be leading tranquil lives, transiting smoothly from one household to the other at regular intervals and be calm, soothing, agreeable animals. The real cats, by contrast, exhaust us with their differences, which get more marked as they get older.

Grace, for example, likes to eat early and go to bed early. Ideally she has dinner at six and by eight she's folded herself elegantly into whatever is her current favoured spot and is focused on getting a sound night's sleep. This is necessary because despite the fact that she gets fed every morning at around quarter to seven, Grace always gears up to breakfast like it's the D-Day landings in Normandy. By four she's awake and has herself stationed outside our door, where she starts counting down the minutes to six, which she regards as the cats' official breakfast time (I'm sure that Grace is convinced that in properly regulated households, cats are fed exactly on the hour at six hourly intervals beginning at midnight). If I wake early I'm conscious of her sitting there, listening and watching and monitoring us. I suspect she can tell when we're awake — I assume our breathing or our movements alter — but Michael and I adhere firmly to the belief that we are not awake *until we open our eyes*.

Grace's aim is to get us to open our eyes as soon as possible. Most mornings start with a scratch on the bedside rug — Grace never claws the bedside rug at any other time of day — so we know this is deliberate noise to wake us. If there's no response from either of us in the next quarter of an hour, she sends in the troops. Kate's usually in the background somewhere. She's never as desperate for breakfast as Grace, but being such a histrionic personality, she can't resist getting involved in any drama that's underway and we are sure Grace knows this. In some cat-to-cat communication, she conveys to Kate that it would be a good idea if she got up onto the bed and checked to see that everything is alright. So Kate leaps up on the bed, trots up and peers at our faces. Familiar with this tactic, we both keep our eyes resolutely closed. Our lack of reaction flummoxes Kate. Sometimes she will give an upset little meow, but mostly she just goes and sits on the windowsill.

This leaves Commander-in-Chief Grace to manage the crisis. She waits another quarter hour and then jumps up onto the bed herself. She inspects Michael's face. She peers at me. Usually by this stage we have to get up in any case, so one or other of us gives a resigned grunt and says, "Okay, I'll feed you."

But occasionally, if we've been out late, or it's the weekend, or it's overcast and dark, we will manage to sleep through all the preliminaries. So Grace will have to take more decisive action. When she gets up on the bed, she walks over both of us and then she nudges me. She smacks Michael on the head with a paw. If this fails, Kate will get called back in to assist on the understanding that two cats simultaneously walking over two people is likely to be more effective than one. And if all these manoeuvres fail, the final, and invariably successful, tactic is The Invasion Of The Bedside Table.

The bedside table is about a foot square and from repeated experience I can now confidently answer the question (in the unlikely event anyone ever thinks to ask it), "How many full-grown cats can you fit on your bedside table?" The answer is, "Two." However, it's important to add, "But, it's not a good idea for them to try and turn around." Which is exactly what they do. Both Kate and Grace get on the bedside table (which has the added advantage from their perspective that it's right at my eye level so they can peer into my face at the same time) and then with their tails projecting in different directions, they turn around. The lamp, the library books, my reading glasses go flying. Quite often, too, there's a magazine on the table, half hanging over the edge, on which Kate takes an unwise step . . .

But what's really galling about these morning campaigns is the reaction of the third member of the trio. The Fluffer is the complete opposite of Grace. She likes to stay up late. She doesn't usually go to bed until just before midnight and even then she often gets up later for a little pre-dawn run-around. As a result, most mornings she's sleepy. While Grace is trying to wake us up, the Fluffer will be at the foot of the bed, curled up in her furs like an heiress who's been out nightclubbing. Two big golden eyes will open and regard the situation. "Breakfast, Fluffer," we'll say to her once her sisters have woken us up. She'll look at us in mild surprise. It's clear that her idea of breakfast is two oysters at around eleven.

At our urging she will follow the other two off to eat, but while they're standing over their bowls chewing away enthusiastically at their dry food, she will be sitting and gazing at her dish, a pensive expression on her face. "Cat food." Quite often she's downstairs and back on the bed in three minutes, having eaten less than a spoonful of breakfast. But some mornings, especially when she's failed to requisition herself a supper of human food the previous evening, she will be hungry and we'll see her sitting looking down at her food, plainly psyching herself up to eat it: "You know you often like it once you get started."

Usually at some stage during a period of feline overwhelmingness, recriminations will break out between Michael and me.

"Your favourite cat," I tell him crossly one morning, "has got a very nasty streak."

I'm getting dressed for work, hurrying between the bathroom and the ironing board, trying to decide what to wear, attempting to hear the weather forecast, swallowing mouthfuls of coffee, and Kate's keeping me company. Helping me get ready for work is a very important part of her day. She bustles about after me, clearly in mother cat mode, supervising my activities and urging me to do things more quickly — except that every now and again she suddenly remembers that me getting dressed means that I'm going away and she does a rapid role switch from mother cat to unhappy kitten, meowing desperately for my attention. As soon as I speak to her or stroke her, she recovers her equilibrium and reverts to being mother cat.

On this particular morning, though, she's unable to bustle around after me because Grace has placed herself at the top of a pair of stairs in the centre of the hall and is stopping her from passing.

"She's intimidating poor Kate," I say. Poor Kate is now backed up against the bedroom door. She knows if she tries to pass Grace, Grace will swipe her. She looks at me with big upset eyes.

Michael's response is to come out of his office, survey the situation, and then stroke Grace's head.

"Kate's just a natural victim," he says indulgently.

Grace rubs her chin lovingly along his hand.

"You're rewarding bad behaviour," I say.

He points out reasonably that he would be perfectly willing to reward good behaviour if the cats ever manifested any.

The situation gets further complicated by the fact that we often have contrasting reactions to each new cat drama. I usually feel inadequate. During one of our overwhelmed periods we go to a party and a pleasant woman enquires how I get on with the trio.

I tell her the truth: "I'm always worried about one of them. I always feel guilty about one of them. And one of them intimidates me."

The pleasant woman doesn't miss a beat. "It sounds like a pretty average family," she says.

After that I give myself lectures. Plans for reform start with Kate and the Fluffer. I tell myself I must stop feeling guilty about one of them and being overprotective towards the other. Guilt reduction turns out to be easier, simply because the Fluffer is always finding new ways of putting herself in danger. She nearly falls off the bedroom windowsill. She has started exploring further and further down the street which joins a busy road and she's always out the front of the house soliciting pats from passers-by.

To stop worrying, I remind myself she's always shown herself to be more competent than I expect. She's never been injured and, while it's true she doesn't appear to use it very often, she does have a brain. Indeed, I've come to the conclusion that the Fluffer's attitude towards mental activity is a bit like mine towards bending over and touching my toes. I know how to do it and I know it would be good for me to do it several times a day. It's just that it doesn't feel comfortable, so I don't often get round to it.

As far as Grace is concerned, I decide that my problem is lack of confidence. One day a visitor to the house picks her up. As usual, Grace growls. She doesn't like being picked up. She doesn't like being carried. She sees no reason why she should be expected to sit on anybody's lap.

"Don't you growl at me, madam," the visitor retorts coolly. "I've got cats at home. They don't treat me in this manner."

A firm hand holds Grace's scruff. She goes quiet. She stays put. I'm very impressed.

"You're not interventionist enough with Grace," I tell myself. "She knows she can put it over on you."

In the evening, I go to the chair on which Grace has seated herself. I pick her up, carry her to my armchair by the heater and place her on my lap.

She doesn't growl but she gives me a look: "Just because I've got the good manners to let myself be strong-armed by people whom you see fit to invite to this house doesn't mean I expect the same treatment from you."

I let her go.

Michael has the opposite reaction to me. He believes it is up to the cats to reform themselves. When we're feeling overwhelmed he announces new stern regimes to modify their behaviour. Most of these, of course, focus on food. This inevitably means confrontations with Grace. When I hear a firm "No you don't!" echoing through the house, I know that he's decided to put another scheme of meal regulation in place.

My response is to be supportive but to try and keep out of the way, because despite months of effort we've never succeeded in convincing Grace that she's entitled to breakfast and dinner and no other meals. She still eats her own portion of breakfast and a fair amount of the other cats' and then settles into her daily campaign to prevent the onset of starvation which she figures will hit her about noon unless she takes urgent action. We go from thinking that her favourite historical character was the person who invented brunch to realising that she regards the entire morning as an extended refuelling session. Being an intelligent cat she's worked out long ago that two people in the house doubles her opportunities for food. She considers Michael her chief provider because he does the cooking, but she knows I can be a useful backstop. Her overtures range from the aggressive to the tender. Sometimes she makes it impossible for us to walk down the stairs. At other times there'll just be a gently insistent brush across the backs of our legs: "I'm here. I love you. How about some lunch?"

Michael's more ambitious schemes for cat reform concern their general behaviour. "They're too dependent on us," he tells me one night. "I've known cats who didn't hang around people all the time. And even though there's three of them, they can't defend themselves. Look at what happens with Tarmac."

Tarmac is the local terror. We have never discovered his real name but christen him one day when we notice how exactly his greyish-black coat matches the surface of the road. He lives in a house several doors up and clearly comes from a long line of hoodlum cats. Every so often he has an idea, "I think I'll go down and stir up those girls in the house on the corner."

The reaction of our cats to his incursions must always be gratifying. Kate, Grace and the Fluffer clearly consider him a cross between Jack the Ripper and Attila the Hun. When I was a child I once heard the racket when a fox literally did get into a henhouse. Tarmac's occasional visits remind me of the incident. There are screams of terror and the sounds of pursuit and flight. Fortunately Tarmac is frightened of Michael and slinks away at the sight of him, but that's no comfort to Michael. With memories of schoolyard bullies and childhood harassments, he wants the cats to organise themselves. Grace has the brains. Kate's got the brawn and the Fluffer's truly lethal when she's in thug princess mode.

"It's because they're females," I say, "and he's a lout."

Tarmac has an over-large head and when I pass him on the street, he looks at me with lazy insolence. I figure he goes out drinking on Friday nights with the biker toms who came to visit Kate when she was on heat.

"I've known other female cats," Michael is saying, "who got together and stopped cats like Tarmac. They're too dependent on us," he reiterates.

To me this sounds suspiciously to me like the line put forward by the Self-reliant cat experts who argue that cats remain perpetual kittens as a result of living with human carers. On the other hand, it does seem a good thing to develop our cats' independence. Unlike many cats whose owners go out to work, they have people in the house most of the day. (We've both had the experience of arriving home and catching a glimpse of them through the window. All three will be sitting placidly together. But within seconds of us coming into the house, they'll be staging something that looks like a crowd fight scene from a kung fu movie interspersed with the final heats of the Olympic three staircase relay.) Also, I'm worrying as usual about the Fluffer. Tarmac hasn't been the only feline visitor recently.

One sunny afternoon Michael and I are on the roof together when we hear an agitated-sounding meow. Concerned, we start calling to the cats, all three of whom eventually appear, get patted, reassure us that there's nothing wrong with them, and then hang around for a wash, a stare into space and the standard range of cat leisure activities. The cry comes again, louder this time, and then a slim young black cat appears over the roof wall.

He's delighted to see Michael and I. He's purring, leaping onto laps, arching himself in pleasure, nuzzling furniture, pressing his head worshipfully against whatever parts of us he can reach and chattering away busily as he does so. "How lovely to meet you! Isn't this a beautiful place! What a wonderful house! How well your pot plants are doing! What a perfect spot for a winter lunch or a summer evening supper!"

Michael and I start to laugh. We've both met this MO before. GB was more laid-back. His manner was affable, gracious, quite seigneurial. But he and this new cat are

Summer/Autumn

alike in that they both project utter confidence and complete self-possession. They could talk their way in anywhere and they both know it. New black cat's a total flirt but he does it so well, it seems boorish of us not to flirt back. We promptly nickname him "Poise".

While Poise's floorshow is underway, our three cats simply sit and stare. It looks to us as though they're flummoxed by his performance. They've never had to talk their way in anywhere. We doubt that any one of the three can flirt. We suspect the idea's never occurred to them. We say to each other it's all very well having the brightest cat in the universe, the most beautiful cat in the universe and the universe's best copycat, but what about a cat with charm? A cat with joie de vivre? A cat who's the life of the party?

Poise trots off after a short time. He's new in the neighbourhood and still has many places to explore, but he lets us know he's thrilled to meet us and will drop back for cocktails later if his owners aren't home. He leaves without any obvious reaction from our cats except that afterwards I find the Fluffer is constantly coming in to visit me. This in itself isn't unusual except that her manner's different. For a cat who's usually sweet and placid, she seems quite intense. Indeed, when she comes in she looks around the room in the same way that Kate does when she's having one of her jealous fits. It's clear she thinks I'm secreting another cat about my person. She's upset with me for flirting with Poise.

I have never seen the Fluffer act like this before and it occurs to me now that perhaps I encourage her dependence on me. I'm keeping her a kitten when she should be a full-grown cat. She's already got Grace looking after her. One mother is enough.

"What do you think we should do?" I ask Michael.

"Well," he says, "they're too underfoot all the time. They could spend more time up on the roof. It's warm and sunny up there most of the day, and in any case there's plenty of shelter."

A few days later when Kate is attacking the blankets as I'm making the bed, the Fluffer is sitting on the fax machine and Grace is trying to extract meal xxiv or xxvi or some other conjunctures of xs that my knowledge of roman numerals is too limited to conceptualise, I decide it's time to put the new stern regime in place. All three cats are seized and carried struggling to the roof. I explain to them that I've put out some food, there's plenty of water and there are nice places to sleep. I'm going out for the afternoon, but Michael will be home in a couple of hours.

As it happens both of us are late — it's dark by the time I get in. Michael's in the kitchen unpacking a large grocery order and I go to help, relieved that I don't have the trio under my feet insisting on dinner, affection and anything else that's available.

"Where are they all?" he asks.

I point upwards, feeling rather pleased with myself. My first thought was to go immediately and let them in but then I remembered. They are all healthy, full-grown and overprotected. They are supposed to be developing their self-reliance.

Michael leaves and reappears a minute later preceded by three cats. "They were very relieved to see me," he says. "It's turned cold —"

"They can go in the sunroom —"

"— and it's gotten dark," he adds. "They didn't even have a candle!"

He delivers this last line like it's one of the all-time heartbreakers, on a par with "I have always relied on the kindness of strangers".

I stare at him in astonishment. Is this the stern new regime in practice?

TEMPLE CAT

As summer turns into autumn I notice that I have less of a tendency to explain about the cat co-owning arrangement. I tell people that we have three cats, we planned to have two and a third arrived and leave it at that. This is partly because Ron and Robin's return keeps getting delayed. Unexpected work and family commitments keep them in Los Angeles through February, March and April, and it seems overly complicated going into detail about these absentee owners. But I also know that I don't talk about the arrangement because I don't want to think about it. Even if the co-owners don't return for months, I know that they will come back and the cats will vanish out of my life. "But only for a time," I always add to myself. Ron and Robin are talking about staying for a year in Sydney when they finally do return, but I'm sceptical. I've never known them to stay for longer than three months and figure that things are unlikely to change.

Summer/Autumn

But when it becomes clear that Ron's work commitments are going to extend into winter, I'm not the only one who starts to get anxious about the arrangement. The cats were supposed to come and go every couple of months, but now they've been with us full time for almost a year. Ron and Robin make jokes in emails about having to climb up onto our roof on their return to abduct the trio, and Michael and Robin predict cheerfully that there will be such a nasty custody war between me and Ron about the cats that they will have to pretend to be enemies while sneaking off for surreptitious cups of coffee together.

One day, not entirely to my surprise, there's a serious proposal. The cats have been with us for so long that the co-owners no longer feel comfortable about expecting the arrangement to continue — would we consider splitting up the cats? The idea is that we would keep Kate and the Fluffer and Ron and Robin will take Grace. My answer is an immediate, "No".

I do this for Grace's sake. One late autumn evening something unexpected happens. I've finished work for the day but go back to my office for my reading glasses and discover Grace asleep on my chair. This is not the unexpected thing. All the cats are equipped with radar screens and teleporting capabilities which mean they can immediately detect and take advantage of any alterations in household arrangements that might contribute to their comfort or happiness. If I place a freshly washed sweater on the bed for Michael to put on when he comes out of the shower, a minute later Kate will be reclining luxuriously upon it — and looking so content, he'll decide to wear something else. If I leave my lunch briefly to answer a phone call, I will find the Fluffer has beamed herself down from a neighbour's roof and is now advancing on my tuna sandwich.

This evening my office is the perfect place for a cat's pre-dinner nap. The chair is warm from me sitting on it and the room is warm from having the heater on. Grace opens her eyes when I come in and I automatically lean over to give her chin a rub. She arches her long neck for my caress and as she does so, I find myself saying, "You're shy aren't you, Grace?"

It comes out quite spontaneously and afterwards I feel a little foolish. It seems silly to go around announcing to cats that they are shy. Also, despite the fact that I'm constantly making up dialogue for the Fluffer and have frequent imaginary conversations with Kate and Grace, I am conscious of the importance of not ascribing human emotions to cats. Furthermore, the insight itself is hardly grand or new. I have always known that Grace is reserved, ever since that first afternoon when she sat and watched us unfamiliar human beings while the Fluffer came up to us for cuddles.

A couple of nights later when the weather turns cold, Grace comes into the bedroom and looks at me thoughtfully. I am sure she remembers getting under the covers when it was cold last winter so I go and pick her up, place her on the bed next to me and pull the blankets up over her. I don't expect her to stay but she sleeps stretched out beside me all night and returns the following evening. I am changing the sheets when she comes in. She doesn't try to leap on the blankets while I'm putting them in place as Kate would, or interrupt me for caresses like the Fluffer.

She just sits and watches what I'm doing, her head at an angle while she follows my movements, and I remember what Michael always says about her: "Grace understands things. You can negotiate with her."

When I'm finished making the bed, she waits for me to get settled and then leaps onto the bed and comes up to me. I lift the blankets so she can slide under while saying, "You're sure you won't get suffocated, Grace?" Then we arrange ourselves comfortably and, with her spine resting against mine, we both go to sleep.

The combination of my sudden insight and her overture transforms my whole relationship with Grace. I stop feeling awkward and inadequate around her. Before long I'm unselfconsciously addressing her as "darling" (which I've always called Kate and the Fluffer) and am saying briskly, "Oh, don't be silly, you know I'm always nice to you!" when she growls at being prevailed upon to do something she doesn't like.

Some time later I become aware that I'd always thought her reserved nature was a matter of choice. I had noted the contradiction between her obviously deep affections and her withdrawn manner, but it had never occurred to me that she might find life as complicated emotionally as she does intellectually. But even before I realise this, I begin to feel as though I understand her. Moreover, I find a context for her.

One morning I see her sitting on the stairs. All three cats often sit on the stairs but Kate and the Fluffer usually sit where they can watch us in our offices. Grace places herself where she can monitor events on both floors as though she is the guardian of the house. Coming down the staircase towards her I notice how elegantly she has arranged herself. She's sitting on all fours with her head on the side and her cheek resting upon her paws. Her eyes are closed but she's alert. It's as though she's in position waiting for a ceremony to begin. As I'm looking at her I can suddenly see generations of cats. They are lined up on the steps of a temple while worshippers file by. They are slender and fine-boned and sit as still as carvings. I stroke her chin admiringly, "Hello, temple cat," I say.

The fact that I've finally bonded with Grace isn't why I say no to Ron and Robin's proposal. The reason I oppose it is because I don't want to part her from the Fluffer. I know that by nature Grace is a solitary cat, but it's also obvious that she remembers and that she feels deeply. The Fluffer has been the one constant presence in her life. She and the Fluffer don't interact affectionately like my imaginary black and white cats. Now they are adults, they only occasionally kiss noses and never curl up together on chairs. But the first time that the Fluffer tries to climb the big tree at the front of the house, we notice Grace is sitting on the roof of a neighbour's car, supervising.

"Grace would suffer the most if they were parted," I say to Michael. "She's the emotionally intense one. The Fluffer would miss her and be a bit lost for a while but she wouldn't mourn for Grace like Grace would mourn for her."

"Also, Grace would worry about her," I add to myself, thinking of what a worrier Grace is and how much I still worry about the Fluffer myself. At the end of my year of living full time with the cats, I'm conscious of the progress

Summer/Autumn

I've made. I've established my relationship with my enigmatic Grace and I've become aware that I don't really need to feel constantly guilty about Kate.

More than this, I have come to realise my guilt about her is not even relevant. Kate is never going to become the serene and equable cat of my imagination, but she's actually quite content in her world. My theory about Kate is that she has inside her head a manual called "How To Be A Proper Cat". Unfortunately, though, several pages of this estimable volume are missing, so her mission in life is to make up for these lost pages by diligently studying the behaviour of the other cats and putting into practice what she learns. As she lacks both Grace's intelligence and agility and the Fluffer's serenity and capacity for pleasure, this is often difficult, but she perseveres nonetheless.

One night, for example, while he's sitting up late watching TV, Michael observes her sleeping on the top of the high-backed armchair which is one of the Fluffer's favourite spots. But Kate's much larger and when she's deeply asleep, she tends to stretch and overbalance. Michael watches in astonishment as she falls off the chair, gets on it again and goes back to sleep once more, only to repeat the exercise half an hour later. He decides that the shock of falling off the chair in her sleep must be negligible compared to the satisfaction she derives from knowing that she is doing what a cat's supposed to do. And she has some successes. After three months of earnest effort she learns to sit on my lap with such a confident air, I see Grace giving her an interested look once as she passes by: "Might try that myself sometime."

The Cat Who Looked at the Sky

But occasionally Kate attempts the impossible. "Surely she can't be trying to get up there!" I exclaim to Michael as I watch her manoeuvring herself onto a narrow space on a bookshelf where the Fluffer sometimes takes a nap. The space is so small that even the Fluffer can't fit onto it properly, except that one of the Fluffer's peculiarities is that she will happily sleep with her head dangling down unsupported, as if her neck's been broken, so it doesn't seem to matter to her that only two-thirds of her body is on the shelf. Kate struggling to squeeze herself into the same tiny area looks like a very large man attempting to get comfortable on a dinner plate. Michael merely glances at her. Unlike me, he's never surprised by any of her excesses. "She's happy, darling," he says. "She thinks she's doing what a cat's supposed to do."

Indeed, Kate's so focused on the whole business of properly being a cat that I'm not even worried about sending her to live with Ron and Robin. I predict she'll be a bit unnerved for the first few hours, but once she realises she is safe, she will start taking her cues from the responses of the other cats and become completely preoccupied with imitating their behaviour. There will be a whole new house full of places to investigate, places to colonise, places to sleep and additionally, in Kate's case, places from which to observe the other cats investigating, colonising and sleeping. I can see her being very stimulated and very busy. Also, I doubt she'll miss me. Although she's a one person cat, the one person is interchangeable. Just as long as there is one. I'm confident she'll bond immediately with Robin and when Robin is not available, start making overtures to Ron.

Summer/Autumn

In all this time, though, I haven't learnt how to stop worrying about the Fluffer. She only has to be a few minutes later than the other cats in appearing for her meals and I'm imagining her knocked down by a car and dead in the gutter. Of all the three cats, she is the most attached to me and I'm anxious about sending her to the co-owners. I imagine her being confused and lonely and wandering around the strange house searching for something familiar. But then I remind myself that the Fluffer can look after herself and I remember two incidents.

The first incident involved our sociable visitor, Poise. One afternoon, a few days after his first visit, Poise comes calling again. "We've got company," says Michael, hearing him meowing on the roof. At the time all five members of the household are gathered in the bedroom, Michael and I are reading and the three cats are asleep — Kate on the bed, Grace on the linen chest and the Fluffer on the rug beside the heater. At his cry, the trio open their eyes. We can see them all processing the information his meows impart. There's that new black tomcat. He's climbed up on the roof again and got in the door. Now he's sitting up on the top landing. At this point Grace and Kate apparently decide that Poise's arrival is a matter of no importance and close their eyes again. The Fluffer appears about to follow suit, or maybe it just takes her longer to work out what things mean because as the other cats are settling down again, she rises to her feet and lopes out of the room.

A few minutes later we hear hissing and go to investigate. Poise is standing on the top landing staring down at the Fluffer, who is hunched down on a stair just below him. She hisses fiercely, making it perfectly clear that while it wouldn't worry her if another half-demented tabby or part-Burmese intellectual wants to join the household, there is only room in this establishment for one charming black cat with big golden eyes and that position, *thank you very much*, is taken.

"Well, it's her house," I say to Michael. "If she doesn't want him, he'll have to stay out." Michael grins and agrees and goes up to give the Fluffer a pat. "I'm very proud of her," he says. We both are. We know she is a great fighter but we've never seen her conduct a campaign like this before. Frankly we never thought she had the concentration. She is also very proud of herself. When Michael stoops to pat her again, she stands up and arches her back for his caress, then instantaneously drops down again to resume full-on hostilities with Poise. Bared teeth, upright fur, high volume hissing.

Poor Poise looks perplexed. Nothing in his considerable experience at ingratiating his way into new households seems to have prepared him for this. He is half on the defensive, sitting up on his hind legs, paws forward ready to divert a swipe, and half convinced that the Fluffer is playing. He keeps looking at her as if to say, "You can't be serious." But the Fluffer is in deadly earnest. She has no intention of backing down. Two hours later as we are sitting down to dinner we can hear Poise calling down to us, "Hey, you guys, how are you? Hasn't it been lovely weather! Thought I'd just drop in for a couple of sauvignon blancs — if somebody could just come up and remove this assassin from the stairs."

The other event also happens on a weekend afternoon. It's later in autumn and the street is covered in golden leaves. I see the Fluffer disappearing out of the sitting room windows and go to the front door to call her back. In addition to being anxious about traffic, I'm always worried now about the Fluffer being out on the street. She has a habit of promenading up and down in front of the house and soliciting pats from passers-by. I've become quite used to seeing the top of a head passing the sitting room windows and then suddenly bobbing out of sight to reappear a few seconds later. But I can't help fearing that one of these days one of the Fluffer's admirers will be tempted to abduct her. She's very pretty and she's very affectionate. I can easily see some passer-by falling in love with her charm and her golden eyes. She could be scooped up and disappear in seconds.

When I call her, the Fluffer's headed down the street. She turns to look at me but keeps on going. It's very still, there's scarcely any traffic on the main road and only a couple of cars are parked in the cul-de-sac, so I decide it's quite safe. And then I see what's attracting her. Down the end of the street a flock of pigeons has landed. They're taking advantage of the quiet to scavenge for food amongst the autumn leaves. They haven't noticed the black cat with her golden eyes moving carefully through those golden leaves towards them.

I start to follow and then stop, amused. I'm suddenly aware of our different views of the world. I'm always frightened when she is out on the street that someone is going to scoop up my little black cat and take her away. But in her mind, the Fluffer is a lioness and she is on the savannah now, moving downhill to her prey.

ONE YEAR LATER

THE CAT WHO
LOOKED AT THE SKY

For months in advance, I prepare myself for the day when the cats are to go to their other home by making plans. I often think about how I will organise bribes, take the trio's favourite foods and toys with us to divert them, and how we'll stay at Ron and Robin's until they are comfortable. I know, of course, that all this is just a way of distracting me from worrying about whether we're doing the right thing. Not to say avoiding thinking about how much we'll miss them and how strange the house will seem when they are gone. Nonetheless by the time departure day arrives, I have rehearsed every detail of the event right down to how Michael and I will make our exits when the cats are settled into their first long sleeps at their other home. On the designated day, though, it turns out

One Year Later

that we're both suddenly and unexpectedly very busy. We don't get an opportunity to stock up on treats for them and neither of us can stay at Ron and Robin's for longer than half an hour. Moreover, we arrive with only two out of three cats.

This last hiccough's my fault. We assemble all the cats' equipment — litter trays, food and feed bowls — well in advance but we leave installing them in their carriers until as late as possible, so as to stop them getting agitated. My job is to round up the cats and incarcerate them while Michael goes to fetch the car. He has had to park blocks away as the street is very crowded. I put Grace in her and the Fluffer's carrier first and she takes the experience quite calmly. Then I put Kate in hers. But as I'm closing the door, the holder that secures it breaks off in my hand. Kate pushes against the door and it promptly falls off. I seize her and put her in the carrier with Grace.

I realise immediately that this was a mistake. I hear growls from Grace and spitting followed by pathetic "How can you do this to me?" meows from Kate. But I've become worried now about the Fluffer, who has realised that something is happening and is about to take flight. I pick her up and carry her into our bedroom where I zip her into a roomy overnight bag. Then I carry both containers downstairs to the front hall.

The Fluffer and Grace are silent which is a relief because Kate keeps up a heartbroken lament loud enough for all three of them. I feel like I'm torturing them. Also, it's becoming clear that nothing is going to go according to plan. The entrance to the street has now been blocked by a large delivery truck which is going to have to manoeuvre slowly into a nearby lane before Michael can bring our car up to the house.

The wait's not very long, but as the minutes pass and Kate wails, I feel increasingly guilty. I begin to think how unkind we are being to them. All three cats should now be settling down to their first morning siesta instead of being shut up in strange places with no idea what is happening. It's while I'm thinking this that it occurs to me that the Fluffer is surprisingly quiet and I begin to wonder if she's getting sufficient air. In retrospect this seems ludicrous. She is a small cat and the overnight bag is large and probably far from airtight, but I decide to open the top zip half an inch just to be sure. I turn away to give Kate a few comforting pats through the rails of the carrier and look around in time to see the Fluffer heading towards the stairs at a businesslike pace. Not running, but walking very fast, clearly determined to put as much distance as possible between her and whatever it is that is going on.

I set off after her, cursing my stupidity. I had looked away for all of a minute and she had managed to push the zip open and escape. But I know I'm not going to catch her. Her usual refuge when there's a disturbance in the house is a shelf on my bedside table but I know she won't go there now. I'm sure that she's gone up to the roof and crawled into the space under the eaves where Grace took her to hide during the carpet laying. It's impossible to see her when she's in there, much less reach in and extract her. I know that she won't come out when I call, she doesn't trust me. She is just going to go to sleep until she decides things are back to normal and it's safe for her to emerge.

I explain all this to Michael when he appears but he sets

One Year Later

off nonetheless to search for her and I follow. We examine each room and walk around the roof, calling to her. There's no response. I say that we could postpone the whole business. Ron and Robin are coming to dinner at our place in a few days. They could collect the trio then. Michael vetoes this. He is all geared up to deliver the cats today. "We'll take Kate and Grace over now," he says. "And when the Fluffer comes out this evening, I'll catch her and take her over." He says this very firmly. I know what he's thinking. The Fluffer is my favourite. He suspects this is a plot to keep her. I don't blame him — I'm beginning to feel myself that I connived in her escape.

The mood in the car during the drive across the city is grim. Michael and I are both worried about how the cats will settle into their other home and our anxiety is increased by the sounds of battle in the cat carrier on the rear seat. Grace and Kate are now thoroughly upset. There is growling and spitting and the carrier gives an occasional lurch when one cat takes a swipe at the other. I can't stop thinking how badly I have managed things. It would have made much more sense to put Kate, as the largest cat, in the overnight bag and transport Grace and the Fluffer together. Grace will always look after the Fluffer whereas she just gets irritated with Kate. At the same time I could have held Kate in her bag on my lap and talked to her. Michael and I arrive at Ron and Robin's house feeling agitated, but they merely laugh at the story of the Fluffer's escape, and it suddenly strikes us both that we are very lucky to have three cats to deliver.

We always lived in dread of an accident. I have a constant scenario in my head of what will happen. One morning, one evening, we'll be calling the cats for their meal and one will be missing. We'll do all the usual things. Call some more and wait. Check all the rooms and cupboards to make sure the missing cat is not locked in somewhere. Call again and wait. Compare notes on past disappearances. Repeat all of the above, then go out and search nearby streets, ask neighbours and passers-by, until finally a cat is located bleeding in a gutter.

But the accident, when it happens, comes without any prelude or warning. It is late one humid January night, after we've had guests to dinner, and we're tidying up. We have both been sleeping badly because of the muggy weather, so we are tired and irritable. Then we realise there's no hot water. I say, not wanting a drama, leave it until the morning, but Michael goes out to check the electricity meter and finds Grace lying moaning on the front verandah. There is blood running out of her mouth and she can't stand up. Her rear right leg is bent and dangling. Despite all the times I have lived through this in my imagination, my first thought is: I can't believe this is happening. Also, I can't believe it's happening to Grace. I feel we had a deal with fate. If she survived her first year, she was to be invulnerable. My next thought is to be relieved, not that she is alive, but that it was this night, of all possible nights, that the hot water system chose to stage its demise. Otherwise we wouldn't have found her until the morning.

As it is there is little we can do for her. It's after midnight, too late to take her to the vet, but we can keep her warm, feed her some milk, talk to her gently, make her a bed on the sitting room floor. She is in her house, with her people. We can't ease her pain but we can help reduce the shock.

One Year Later

Early next morning when we come downstairs to check her, she has disappeared. We realise she'll have gone to hide under the desk. When I squat down to look at her, she tries to stand. The movement obviously hurts and she starts to growl quietly, trying to defend herself from the pain. "Poor little cat," says Michael sadly. We feel desperately sorry for her but remind ourselves of the good things. She is conscious. She can sip milk. She knows us. She has a broken leg but she's young and strong. And, as Michael says, she has spirit. Despite the shock and pain of the accident, she managed to drag herself from the street across the footpath and up onto the relative safety of the verandah.

The vet says there is a massive fracture of her upper leg. He thinks she's had a fall but we can't believe that our Grace with her perfect balance could fall from anywhere in her familiar environment on a clear fine night. We think she's been sideswiped by a car and thrown against the gutter. Either way, we know we have been lucky and promptly announce a change in household arrangements to Kate and the Fluffer. "You can go on the street during the day," I tell them, "but come nightfall, you're staying indoors." I really want to stop them going out on the street altogether, but feel this is too much of a curtailment. Also, there's a notice at the vet's that begins: "Most animals are injured after dark ..."

Grace has surgery and spends a week in the animal hospital. A pin is inserted in her leg. The vet says that her heart is strong and he's confident she will recover, so I don't realise how badly injured she is until we're being shown the x-ray of her fracture and I'm suddenly aware that Michael has done a quick retreat backwards across the room and is now seated on a chair in the corner. His face is the same pasty colour as the surgery walls. I can't read an x-ray but he's seen immediately what's happened. The vet runs his finger along the break and explains to me that the bone has been smashed and fragmented at the edges of the fracture. It's likely she'll have one leg shorter than the others and will always limp. I think about our clever Grace and how proud we were of her speed and her vertical leaps. Then I remember the important thing.

"How much pain is she in?" I ask.

"We'd prefer she stayed here," intervenes Michael firmly from the corner, "where you can give her something if she's suffering than take her home where we can't help her."

The vet is reassuring and his assistants, as we leave the surgery, are equally reassuring. Young cats mend quickly, we're told by one. Even old cats, says another, are amazingly resilient. Working in an animal hospital announces a third (as he's totting up the bill for the impressively long list of treatments Grace has received), you get to really understand the saying about cats and nine lives. We don't believe a word of it until we get her home and discover that in the briefest of instants Grace can transform herself from frail invalid to top flight athlete.

The plan is for her to convalesce in the sunroom on the roof. It's been stripped of furniture because the vet says that she mustn't climb, jump or run up stairs for the first week after leaving the hospital. Once we get home, though, we feel it's cruel to shut her away immediately. We agree that she needs some special attention and put her down to rest for a while on the bed between the two of us. She plays her part as the wounded heroine beautifully. In pain, but very brave. She accepts some milk from a proffered saucer. Licks a paw. Purrs when we gently stroke her chin while making sure not to go near any of the bruised parts of her jaw. Then she carefully eases herself into a comfortable position and dozes off. We watch her as she lies there between us, apparently deeply asleep, her injured side exposed. Half the hair is shaved off and there's a great curved gash full of stitches across her thigh. Then the phone rings. We both glance towards it and in that microsecond while our attention's distracted, Grace leaps off the bed and tears up the stairs.

We race off after her with visions of stitches ripping, steel pins popping out and hips getting dislocated, but she seems unaffected by her adventure. We find her sitting calmly on the roof with her good side facing us so that it looks as if nothing's happened. Her attitude seems to be: "I don't know what you're all carrying on about. I've got three perfectly good legs and I bet I am still the fastest cat in the neighbourhood." After this display she gets sealed into the sunroom with the sort of security arrangements usually reserved for terrorist suspects wanted by police on five continents.

Although she doesn't like being confined, Grace adapts quite well to her imprisonment because she soon discovers that it comes with a bonus: room service. For a cat whose whole life revolves around food, the idea of being able to eat without any effort whatsoever, of just being able to stretch over from her cushion and take a mouthful of milk or a nibble of meat whenever she feels like it, is as close to heaven as she can imagine. Also, we're so keen to comfort her that we are constantly changing and replenishing her food dishes. The only real indication we have of how much pain she's in is whether or not she eats and on the few occasions that she's not interested in food, we feel so sad we try to devise special treats for her. Mostly, however, she's our own insatiable Grace who looks up bright-eyed at the prospect of every meal.

The week that Grace spends in hospital is the first time that she and the Fluffer have ever been apart. While Kate doesn't appear concerned about her absence, after a couple of days we find the Fluffer sitting in the front hall, gazing at the door. In the Fluffer's happy little universe, periods of distress usually only last the minute or so it takes for her to recover from whatever has surprised or upset her. We have never seen her sitting around looking worried before. Indeed, we don't think she's ever had to. She's always had Grace at hand to do her worrying (along with most of her other mental activities) for her. It's also obvious in this crisis, though, that the Fluffer doesn't have the temperament to be an anxious cat. Compared to how fraught Grace and Kate can get, she doesn't seem especially upset, just sort of wistful and a bit puzzled.

But this display of concern doesn't influence her behaviour when Grace comes back. The first time we let her in to visit Grace, the Fluffer takes one look at her and hisses vehemently.

"Fluffer!" we both say, startled.

The Fluffer hisses again. Grace is standing with her injured leg projecting awkwardly and it's clear the Fluffer doesn't like the strange-looking leg and wants it to go away.

Grace meanwhile gazes at her with a patient, kindly

One Year Later

expression. She seems unsurprised at the Fluffer's response and doesn't appear to regard it as hostile. Michael strokes Grace while I pick up the black cat and soothe her. In typical Fluffer fashion, however, once she's over her initial shock, she seems to forget the whole business.

Kate is the complete opposite. After the Fluffer's reaction, we're careful about her first meeting with Grace, but apart from staring a bit, she seems unaffected and it's a few days before we realise how upset she is. When she takes to sleeping under the wash basin cupboard in the bathroom, we think at first it's because of the hot weather. So while her new favourite place looks uncomfortable — she's squeezed herself into a narrow gap between the bottom of the cupboard and the floor — we decide that perhaps the tiles are cool, or maybe there's a current of air coming in from the stairwell. Often we forget she's there until we're cleaning our teeth at the sink and feel her tail brushing gently over our toes.

Then we begin to notice that she's spending all her time in her strange little retreat. She comes out for meals and then immediately returns to her hideaway. And she's always in the same pose. If I squat down to peer at her, I'll see her lying on her side, facing the door, eyes staring intently back at me. She doesn't look like a cat settling in for a nap in her current favourite sleeping spot. She looks like she's braced for trouble.

We realise her behaviour's linked to Grace's injury but think it will stop once Grace is allowed out. However when, after her week of isolation, Grace is taken to the vet for her check-up, pronounced to be progressing satisfactorily and permitted to resume normal life, Kate still keeps to her refuge. After a further couple of days I decide enough's enough. I go to the bathroom, lift Kate out from under the sink, carry her out, shut the door firmly and put her down in the hall outside.

Her reaction is immediate. The instant her feet touch the ground, she's off. As though propelled out of a gun she hurtles across the hall and into Michael's office where she tears into a corner and squeezes herself into another tiny space atop a pile of magazines at the bottom of a bookcase. I stare in astonishment. Michael bursts out laughing. "Well, at least she's out of the bathroom."

Changing her refuge has no effect on her behaviour. If anything she becomes more obsessive about her new hiding place than her old one. Previously she'd always come out to join the others when we called the trio for their meals, but now I sometimes have to go into the office, lift her out of the bookshelf and carry her up to the food dishes. Once there, she eats and drinks and uses the litter tray, but her manner is subdued and she returns immediately to her cramped refuge. I try nursing her, petting her, brushing her, talking to her, but nothing seems to make an impression. Also, she doesn't seem interested in the other cats, about whose activities she's usually intensely curious. I find myself getting nostalgic for the mornings, only ten days ago, when she would irritate me by hanging around my feet alternately purring and meowing loudly while I was trying to get ready for work.

Radical interventions make no difference. If we shut her out of the office she scrabbles so desperately at the carpet to get in that eventually we have to open the door. If we shut her out of the house altogether, she bolts back into her hiding place the instant that she's allowed back inside. Michael says he finds her presence rather spooky. When he's sitting at his desk he's always aware of her, hunched down in her little space, staring outwards with her big black-rimmed eyes. She scarcely seems to sleep. She always looks tense. Obviously there's some terrible force at loose in the world that is maiming cats and Kate is waiting for it to attack her.

After a couple more days we realise we can't let this behaviour go on. If Kate had something physically wrong with her, we would never allow her to wait around in pain. She is clearly now in mental turmoil and there's nothing we can do to help her. Perhaps the vet can suggest some behaviour modification or give her a calmative. As I'm waiting on the line to make an appointment for her, I start counting up the days. It's nearly two weeks since Grace came home from hospital, Kate's been acting strangely ever since. I'm ashamed we have let her continue in this state for so long.

The night before I'm due to take Kate to the vet, I get woken by the sounds of a cat skirmish in the stairwell. It's just after twelve. I get up immediately to go and check that Grace is alright. We worry about the other cats hurting her in their occasional night-time brawls.

But everything is quiet again by the time I reach the stairs. When I turn on the lights, none of the cats is around. Before setting off upstairs to find Grace, I peer into Michael's office expecting to see Kate's big eyes staring at me from her corner. To my surprise she's not there. It's the first time in a week I have seen her space empty and I'm interested to note that, despite her upset, she appears to be participating in whatever altercation is taking place between the trio. I go up to the roof to look for them but all three have disappeared. There's no moon. I can't see a thing and none of the cats, not even the Fluffer, who's usually solicitous, comes when I call. I say to myself, "Oh well, Grace knows how to look after herself. Go back to bed."

I'm awake by five and hurry upstairs again to ensure that Grace is okay. This time I don't look into Michael's office first to check on Kate and then discover, when I get to the roof, that I don't need to. She's with the other cats. All three are hanging around their food dishes ostentatiously looking forward to breakfast. I point out that officially their dining room doesn't open until six, but on rare occasions I'm prepared to make an exception. Half a minute later I'm gazing at the happy sight of three very different heads lowered over three food dishes and three very different tails — one large and fluffy, one slender and elegant, and one broad and striped — projecting straight upwards into the air.

I go downstairs and report to Michael that Kate is with the other cats and that during the night she left her hidey-hole for a while. He's too sleepy to pay much attention. I fetch the papers, make some coffee and return to bed. But every quarter of an hour I get up to check that (a) Kate has not returned to her corner and that (b) she's still up on the roof doing normal type things with the other cats. (By normal type things I mean washing, eating and sitting looking at whatever it is that cats sit and look at so intently for such long periods of time.) And every quarter of an hour I find to my delight that her behaviour in regard to (a) and (b) is entirely satisfactory. She's washing, eating and looking at whatever it is that cats look at in the most exemplary fashion imaginable.

At six forty-five I wake Michael properly and tell him the news. At seven o'clock I start thinking about cancelling Kate's nine o'clock appointment. At seven-thirty I decide to cancel. At seven forty-five I tell Michael. At eight o'clock I ring the vet's surgery, apologise for the late notice but say my cat seems much improved.

"I can't believe it," I say to Michael. "How come she chose to get better on the exact day I was taking her to the vet?" For it's soon clear that Kate is herself again. She never returns to Michael's office. She seems to have forgotten her trauma. It's as though that whole stage of her life never happened. At ten o'clock when all the cats are settled down to their first major morning sleep, I come across her curled up in an empty clothes basket with the Fluffer. The duo — the Fluffer all in black and Kate in contrasting greys and browns — look like they're posing for a photograph in a cat calendar. Except that they are in the wrong hemisphere. This is a pose for a northern winter, not a steamy Sydney February.

"Aren't you hot?" I ask Kate, who opens her eyes as I'm peering down at them. The Fluffer doesn't stir. She always sleeps deeply in the morning, otherwise I suspect she'd have become uncomfortable and taken herself off to somewhere cooler. I'm partly astonished, partly mystified. It seems to me that Kate is ostentatiously playing mother to demonstrate her recovery. As I watch she curls herself protectively around the Fluffer and then gazes up at me proudly with what I can only describe as a "Tell Mr de Mille I'm ready for my close-up" look on her face.

I find myself feeling a little spooked. I can't stop thinking about the coincidence of Kate getting better the very morning I was about to take her to the vet. For a minute I find myself wondering if she overheard my phone call. Then I remember that I made the appointment while I was at work and there is no way she could have heard me making a telephone call from six suburbs away, but it doesn't stop me wondering.

The previous year when I was in my cat book reading stage, I'd come across various accounts of inter-species communication and pets with apparently paranormal sensitivities. My view is that while I'm prepared to accept there are cats with unexplained mental powers, I believe there's a broad spectrum of talent amongst cats in regard to telepathy, as with other capacities. I do accept the accounts I've read of cats who know when their owners are coming home. But at the same time I've been acquainted with cats who don't appear to recognise their owners if they unexpectedly meet them in the street.

I also feel I know how our cats would react if I were to raise the subject with them. If I were to say to the Fluffer, "There are cats who know when their owners are coming home," she would give me a look of polite incomprehension: "That's nice for them, I guess." Grace would be irritable and point out that this summed up all the problems about being a cat. What possible use would it be knowing what time your owners were coming home if you couldn't influence them to come

One Year Later

home earlier so they could feed you sooner? Kate would be astonished I could be taken in by such transparent behaviour. "Some cats," I can hear her saying, "will do anything for attention."

But now I keep thinking, just after midnight. On the very day we were going to take her to the vet ... It begins to occur to me that it would make sense for Kate to be the one with the telepathic capacities. She is the cat with the practical feline skills. She's the best mouser (which isn't saying much when the total kill at this stage is three and a very small half). She's the best at opening doors; she recognises the sound of our footsteps in the street and ever since she was a kitten she's known how to get into the dry food, which we now have to store away from her depredations in screw-top jars. She is nowhere near as bright as Grace, who understands cause and effect and can hit a key on Michael's computer that makes a bell ring. But Grace, despite Kate's many demonstrations, has never learned how to bite and claw her way into a carton of dry food. I reflect that for a cat there is perhaps no difference between the paranormal and the ordinary. Apprehending a human thought might be no different from working out how to bounce against a door until it swings ajar.

Later, though, I develop another less dramatic explanation for the timing of Kate's recovery. I begin to notice that two weeks is about the time it takes for the cats to adapt to major changes in their lives. And Kate, being a cat who likes to do things properly, would naturally follow the two week rule with such precision that she would stage her return to normality just as midnight on the fourteenth day became morning on the fifteenth. I decide it was only coincidence that this was the same day I was going to take her to the vet.

The fracture in Grace's leg heals very slowly. Each month we take her to the vet and each month he says, "It's getting better but it was such a bad break, I think it needs more time." So the pin stays in. Like a sensible cat, she knows her limits. She is clearly aware she can't manipulate the stiff-pinned rear leg so she never tries to climb the lattice walls around the roof garden, whereas once she used to tear up them as easily as she'd race up the stairs. It's several weeks before she does relatively easy jumps up onto tables. Also, the injury affects her in various unexpected ways. She has trouble leaning over the food dishes to eat, so she takes to dining while lying on her side like a lady reclining at a banquet in Ancient Rome.

She also continues to experience pain occasionally. Mostly it's not clear what causes this. We assume there's been a brawl or running about during the night but it also seems that travelling in the car and being physically examined hurts her too because each trip to the vet is followed by a period of quiet and, on one occasion, she disappears. This happens with dramatic timing because it occurs on the very night that Ron and Robin are flying westwards, after months and months of delays, across the Pacific to finally take up residence back in Sydney.

Michael wakes me very early in the morning: "I can't find Grace."

I say, "It'll be alright, she'll come out for breakfast."

One Year Later

He says with emphasis, "I've put out their breakfast. I've called to her. She hasn't come."

I stare at him. This is a crisis. I find myself remembering one afternoon a few weeks previously when, after several days of hot weather, it was cool and overcast and all five residents of the house had long sleeps. Grace didn't wake until it was quite dark. She suddenly sat upright on our bed with a terribly urgent look of her narrow intelligent face. "I've overslept! It's nearly seven o'clock. Good heavens, I could have starved to death!"

I tell myself not to panic.

"It's still early. She's probably gone off somewhere — she's starting to get about the place a bit more."

"No," he says, "it's more than that. I couldn't find her last night either."

This jolts me. Grace usually spends her nights in one of three or four places, so she's quite easy to find. If she's not at the foot of the bed, she's in the office. If she's not in the office, she'll be on the top landing. If she's not there, she'll be curled up on a dining room chair.

"You'd already gone to sleep, I just wanted to check she was okay," Michael explains. "I looked everywhere. I couldn't find her."

He sits down heavily on the bed. We count up the hours. She was last sighted about eight, on a dining room chair, having a wash and being careful with her injured leg. It was obvious to us that she was in pain because she ate relatively little dinner and was sitting very quietly. But on previous occasions she had always recovered within a few hours. Certainly by next morning she'd be on the bed, waking us up, and then accompanying us to the food

The Cat Who Looked at the Sky

bowls where, while we were getting her breakfast out, she'd stage a three-legged performance of her now famous solo ballet, :"The Famish'd Cat".

"I've looked —" he says and stops. Then he says, "I think she's had a bad turn. Perhaps a heart attack."

"You think she's gone off somewhere to die?"

"Yes."

It's what Mothercat, his old favourite cat, did. She came into the room where he was working, looked at him and then disappeared. He realised afterwards that she'd come in to say goodbye.

I don't want to believe it but after searching the house and the street and the lanes nearby, I begin to realise it could be true. When we can't find her after a couple of hours, I have no choice but to go to work. By this time we know Ron and Robin's plane will have landed and they will be on their way to their house.

"What are you going to say if they ring?"

"Tell them the truth."

He says he'll ring me if there's any news and I get ready to set off for my train thinking sadly, well, we just have to accept it. We had her for two years. We can't replace her. That is how it is. I give Kate and the Fluffer warm pats goodbye thinking, we've still got them. But they seem diminished somehow. Grace was our star. The thought of not seeing her thin intelligent face and big bright eyes again is devastating.

For the first few hours I'm at my office I try resolutely to put the matter out of my mind while glancing every couple of minutes at the phone and praying for it to ring. Finally, desperate for some sympathy, I say, "Our clever cat, the one who was injured, has disappeared. She's never done this before. We think she might have had a heart attack."

Fortunately not a single person in my office believes this theory. Someone points out that she's young and healthy. Someone else recounts how their cat hid away for two days when it was sick. Someone else says their cat came back after a much much longer absence. My spirits begin to lift. I look at the phone confidently expecting it to ring. When it doesn't I pick it up and dial.

It's answered by Michael, sounding flustered. "Yes, she's here," he says. "I don't know where she was. There was someone at the door doing a charity collection and I looked around and there she was. Just standing in the hall near the kitchen, looking fine. I was about to ring you when the doorbell went again and —"

Later he remembers how she just appeared in the hall and realises that she must have been in the cupboard under the stairs. We'd looked there and moved some things around but without much conviction. Although Kate and the Fluffer had hidden in there during their first days in the house, we had never known Grace to go in there except for a one-off walk around and explore. By that stage, too, we were giving up and so, human-like, we had forgotten about the small dark space right at the end, underneath the bottom-most stair, which would be the perfect place for a cat trying to hide away from its pain.

Within a few minutes of our arrival at Ron and Robin's with Grace and Kate, I'm actually relieved that the Fluffer hasn't come because I find introducing the other two cats to their new surroundings sufficiently demanding. This is despite the fact that Grace seems to adapt quickly. She comes out of the carrier, takes a cautious look around and then immediately does a quick investigative tour: all upstairs rooms, all downstairs rooms, after which she has a nibble of food and a wash, followed by another more thorough survey of the premises. We can never know whether she has retained some memories of her old home. It's been so extensively rebuilt since she was last here nearly two years ago — floors replaced, rooms changed, staircase relocated — that it seems unlikely any familiar smells can remain. But perhaps there are other ways she can recognise the place because we notice that when she goes upstairs the second time, she goes immediately to sit in Ron's studio where she spent so much of her kittenhood.

Kate is entirely different. While Grace is exploring, Kate hides. She crawls under Ron and Robin's dining table and stays there until, feeling that she needs some reassurance, Ron and I go to coax her out. She comes out when I call and rubs herself around my legs, meowing loudly. "Poor Katie Kate," I say sadly.

I can see she's very distressed and I'm belatedly realising that I have forgotten the first thing I ever knew about her. That first evening when she came up to our dining room windows, desperate for food and attention, I'd apprehended immediately that she was the sort of cat who fixates on her normal surroundings. And unlike the Fluffer, who changed as she developed, Kate has never altered. This is a cat who's never gone and sat on a neighbour's porch. She goes out onto the street but never for very long and never very far. It's clearly a matter of duty rather than inclination. Her only adventuring is across the roofs of nearby houses, and I suspect she regards our neighbours' roofs pretty much as an extension of our rooftop space. Home territory, like an above-ground backyard.

And now she's in a completely new place and she hates it. She's not hostile to Ron and Robin, she accepts their petting willingly, but she wants her unfamiliar surroundings — different floors, walls, furniture — to disappear. I try to soothe her by giving her a brush.

"Poor Katie Cat," I say. "It'll be alright, don't worry." Kate wails a loud and miserable reply.

Meanwhile Ron, who's been standing watching her, suddenly says delightedly, "Amber. She's amber."

Both Kate and I look at him in surprise. "I'd always thought of her as grey and brown," he says, "but she's amber."

I peer at Kate and realise he's right. She has whorls of colour: dark greys, lighter greys, browns and another colour which I've always thought of as ginger until I look at her now and see that it's got a golden tone, as though there's a light behind it. Amber.

"You're a very pretty cat," he tells her.

Kate's not so distressed that she can't hear the admiration in his voice. She's pleased to come across a human being with the discernment to appreciate her finer points, and she bustles over to respond to his praise with a rub around his legs. I can hear her thinking, "I know you people say Grace is beautiful but have you really looked at her? Whoever did her colouring made a total mess of it. She's mostly black on one side, nearly all tan on the other

— you could be looking at two completely different cats! And the detailing! That stripe on her nose is the queerest thing I've seen. There's a break in it two-thirds of the way up and it's a sort of pinkish whitish colour. Whereas I . . . "

She doesn't have to spell it out. All her stripes and curves and whorls of colour are mathematically exact. Her chin's impeccably snowy. Her eyes are outlined in black. Her face is a series of lovely markings set off by perfect whiskers. They might make brighter cats, they might make more beautiful ones, but she's the very model of a proper tabby cat, and she knows it.

When Ron leans down to pat her, she purrs and then settles into a routine where she goes from one of us to the other, alternately purring and meowing. I'm relieved to see I was right about one thing. She's quite accepting of other human beings. Her focus is on me but I feel sure that when I'm gone, she'll switch her attentions to Ron and Robin. There's nothing for it but for Michael and I to go and leave her to settle in her own time.

We ring that evening to find out how she is and learn she has spent the afternoon hiding in a cupboard in Ron's studio. Next morning the news is better. She's still in hiding but she's spent the night at the foot of Ron and Robin's bed, and she does come out for meals and to use the litter tray. She's clearly just not ready to engage with a strange house.

All this makes me more apprehensive about sending the Fluffer over to join the other two. By the time we both return home that evening, she has come out of hiding and is her normal affectionate self. The morning's dramas seem to have been deleted from her memory bank. She

One Year Later

appears not to have noticed the disappearance of the other cats. We get a reprieve on her departure because everyone agrees there has been enough drama for one day. Ron and Robin will collect her when they come to dinner a couple of nights later.

The Fluffer spends the intervening time exactly as she usually does — until the last morning before she is due to be collected, when I hear a sort of scrabbling coming from the storage space underneath the stairs.

"Fluffer?" I ask. "Fluffer?"

There's no reply and she doesn't emerge but the noise stops. Apart from our second day in the house when Kate took her in there to hide, I've never known the Fluffer to go into the understairs storage. But then I'd never seen Grace go in there either, before her disappearance. I'm beginning to perceive that the space under the stairs is where the cats go when they are perturbed or in pain. I get the message. Any plans I might have been fomenting to keep my favourite with me and let the other two cats come and go between the two households are quickly abandoned. I know it's time the Fluffer rejoined her sisters.

On the night she leaves, she cries so unhappily in the pet carrier that I have to consciously stop myself thinking about a weekend recently when we stayed away overnight. We put out plenty of food for the cats and when we came back, Grace and Kate were happy enough to see us, but otherwise didn't seem to have noticed we'd been gone for longer than usual. The Fluffer, though, was desperately glad to have us back. She purred and rubbed and pressed her cheek ardently against every part of us that she could reach. When I went to bed, she followed Michael around

The Cat Who Looked at the Sky

for the rest of the evening, clearly terrified to let him out of her sight in case he staged another departure.

"The poor Fluffer," we say to each other frequently the next day, "the poor Fluffer, I wonder how she is." But when we ring in the evening we realise we need never have worried. In her new environment the Fluffer goes into lioness mode. When she arrives at the new house, she simply stages one of her standard midnight run-arounds in the course of which poor Kate gets chased from her hideaway under the bed. Next morning she sets off, her tail high, to explore the neighbourhood.

Two weeks later, it's reported that all the cats have settled. The Fluffer continues to appear unaffected by the move. After a week Kate stops hiding and joins the household. She starts taking walks in the garden. Each day Grace grows visibly more confident and relaxed. The vet finally declares that her leg is better and the pin is removed. When the co-owners go to collect her afterwards, Ron nurses her on his lap in the car. To his surprise, she starts to purr. He tells us happily, "She knew she was going home."

And it's two weeks also before I start to miss them. In the first days after they go I expect to feel unhappy but their presence seems so strong in the house that I'm always looking around thinking I will see them. Each time the curtains in the sitting room move in the breeze I see the Fluffer coming in from one of her meet-and-greet sessions on the front footpath. Each time I fold the rug at the foot of the bed I see Kate arriving to place herself precisely in the centre of it.

And whenever I go up the stairs to the roof I see Grace

lying on the top landing as she used to do on late summer afternoons before her accident. She'd lie on her spine with all four legs in the air and her head positioned so that she could flick a glance downstairs to Michael's office in case there was any movement that might signify dinner. But mostly she'd just lie there with all four paws aloft and her big eyes staring skywards in a state of perpetual surprise at being a cat.

EPILOGUE

The cats are now all four years old. The Fluffer, to our relief, has outgrown her daily bouts of aggression towards the other cats. But we're never going to be able to prove our claim that she's the most beautiful cat in the universe because she has added cameras to the list of things — beginning with vacuum cleaners — with which she refuses to deal, and disappears at the sight of one. We've also grown better (or so we think on our optimistic days) at relating to Kate and now, for example, when she has a fit of panic and retreats under the bed, Michael finds he can sit down on the floor next to her and quietly talk her out of her fright. Grace has recovered from her accident but walks with a marked limp. She's adapted to her injury, though, and can run very quickly on three legs with the shortened leg held off the ground and projecting outwards like a handle. Despite her injury too, she can still climb and leap better than either of the other cats.

One Year Later

She is also the only one of the trio who understands about the co-owning arrangement. This still continues, though for a number of reasons it has never been the smooth, frequent transiting we first thought it would be. Instead, the cats tend to stay with both households for long periods of time — nine months with us, then four months with Ron and Robin. When the cats go from one home to the other, we know that Kate and the Fluffer recognise their surroundings straight away, because if they get any shocks or surprises in the tentative few minutes after they first arrive, they will both immediately dash off to some hiding place they established on a previous stay. But they usually get over their nervousness in a couple of hours. By dinner time they'll be taking their places at their food bowls, and then going off to resume their favourite sleeping positions on our beds.

Grace, though, never hides. She steps out of the pet carrier, surveys her domain, rubs around the legs of whichever co-owners she's just been reunited with and then settles down to supervising her new household.